See You on a Starry Night

ALSO BY LISA SCHROEDER

See You on a Starry Night

BY LISA SCHROEDER

SCHOLASTIC INC.

ISBN 978-1-338-28097-5

10 9 8 7 6 5 4 3 2 1   18 19 20 21 22
Printed in the U.S.A.   40
First printing 2018
Book design by Yaffa Jaskoll

This book is dedicated to children affected by divorce.

If that's you, here's a list of things I want you to know:

1. It's not your fault.
2. You are amazing.
3. It's okay to be sad or angry sometimes.
4. Reading books helps. (I know from experience.)
5. A lot of people care about you, including me!

One

NEW HOME

Casper, my old, white kitty, sat perched on my nightstand, studying me like I might unpack a can of tuna any second. Poor cat. No tuna here, just all of the moving boxes marked *Juliet*.

"I'm sorry, sweet boy, but you have to move." I picked him up and kissed the top of his head before placing him on my green-and-purple striped quilt. I only had a couple of boxes left to unpack. I'd already made my bed, unpacked my books and put them in the bookcase, and filled the drawers of my dresser and desk. Now I reached into the box that held pictures and posters and pulled out a framed family photo taken at my eleventh birthday party last August.

As I put the photo down in its spot right next to my bed, I studied it and felt a pinch in my chest. Mom, Dad, my older sister, Miranda, and I all wore pointy red-and-blue hats and had party horns in our mouths. The picture captures a quick moment of a fun and busy day. Besides making

1

me feel pretty ridiculous, the hat's elastic strap had dug into my chin a little, so I hadn't worn it long. None of my friends had, either. Well, except my best friend, Inca. She wore it the entire time because she's nice like that. Pretty sure she didn't want to hurt my feelings, even though the hats weren't my idea in the first place. I'd only bought them because Dad had practically insisted on them and the horns when we went to the party store for invitations.

"Dad, no," I'd said when he took them off the rack. "I'm too old for those."

"Nonsense," he'd said. "A party isn't a party without them."

Mom had spoken up in my defense. "Bruce, if she doesn't want—"

He didn't let her finish. "What's the harm in getting them for people who want to wear them? It's a *party*. We should have hats and horns. End of story."

I'd glanced around, hoping no one was watching us. I hated when they argued in public. Hated it so much. But for once, I could put a quick end to it. "Okay, okay, let's just go."

When Mom showed me the photo, I couldn't believe how happy we all looked. I asked if I could have a copy framed.

Now I loved it even more, because not only had we been happy, we'd also been together. A family.

I'd have worn one of those silly red-and-blue hats every day if it meant we didn't have to move away from everything I'd ever loved. As if my parents' split wasn't bad enough, my mom had to freak out and move us four hours from the town where we'd always lived, and right in the middle of the school year.

Moving meant I had to say so long to the house I'd grown up in, to the art studio that had become like a second home, and to my favorite librarian, Mr. Richie. He gave me a bookmark with his picture on it so I wouldn't forget him. At least that was one good-bye that made me laugh. Before I walked out of the school library for the last time, he told me, "Remember, Juliet, just like in books, everything usually works out in the end. And if it doesn't, that means you simply haven't reached the end yet."

So here we were, in the old red cottage with faded white shutters at Mission Beach in San Diego. My grandparents have owned the rental house for years. We'd stayed here once, on vacation when I was five or six. My grandma had wanted to do some renovations in between long-term renters, so we came for a week before they started the work. Never in a million years had I imagined *living* here. First of all, it's really small. Second of all, it's really far away from the place I've always known as home—Bakersfield. And third, living on the beach always seemed to me like something mostly old people do when they retire.

Not that I don't love the beach. I do. But living there year-round? I just wasn't sure if I wanted sand in my life, in my fingernails, and in my underwear 365 days a year.

"How long are we staying?" I'd asked my mom.

"Indefinitely," she'd replied.

That is one word that will never make it onto one of my favorite word lists. It's so useless. Why not just say *I don't know*?

Anyway, the house. My old room was double the size of this new one, and even worse, all three of us would be sharing one teensy-tiny bathroom. At least I had the freezing-cold ocean nearby to bathe in if we ran out of time in the mornings and I didn't get my turn, right?

I know what you're thinking. Why in the world am I complaining about living at the beach? The thing is, we could have been moving into Cinderella's castle at Disneyland and I still would have been sad. Okay, well, maybe not *too* sad. Dole Whips in my backyard? Yes, please! But you know what I'm saying. Moving away—from your neighborhood, your school, your friends, your father—is hard. Plus, our family wasn't a whole family anymore. I'd heard adults use that term "from a broken home," but I'd never really understood what it meant. Until now. When your parents break up, everything feels kind of . . . broken.

Mom and Dad decided Miranda and I would visit Dad once a month in Bakersfield, and spend part of summer and winter breaks with him, too. I just kept telling myself I'd see him, and hopefully my friends as well, every time we went back there.

Still, it was a lot of changes at once. In one week, at the end of spring break, I'd have to start at a new school in the middle of the year when everyone but me knew how to find their classrooms and who to sit with in the cafeteria. All I'd have was a book with Mr. Richie's bookmark to keep me company. Maybe the art room or the library would be open at lunch. I could only hope.

If only Mom had been willing to wait until the end of the school year to move. But she'd insisted that we needed to do it now. When I'd asked her why, she'd just said, "Trust me, Juliet, it's for the best."

Best? But why? And for who?

After I unpacked my boxes and hung up my favorite poster, Vincent van Gogh's *The Starry Night*, I asked Mom if we could go down to the beach. She was busy putting dishes away in the kitchen cupboards.

"I can't go with you now, but maybe Miranda can."

"No!" my sister called from her room.

My sister loves me a whole lot, as you can tell.

"Can I go by myself?" I asked.

"I don't know, honey," Mom said.

"What's the point of living near the beach if I can't, you know, *go to the beach*?" I asked. "If all we wanted was to listen to the sound of waves, we should have bought one of those fancy sound machines."

"She has a point," Miranda called out.

Was that my sister, actually taking my side? What a miracle. I watched as Mom reached into a box of crumpled-up newspaper and pulled out a stack of plates.

"Oh, all right," she said. "Just for a little while. Take my phone with you, just in case. If something happens, call Miranda immediately, all right?"

"You know, if I had my *own* phone . . ."

Mom gave me her "Don't go there" look.

"It's two o'clock on a Sunday," I said. "The beach is going to be packed. What could possibly happen?"

She looked at me. "Honey, a lot of things can happen, unfortunately. Please don't go in the water by yourself. And don't talk to strangers. And—"

"Don't get into creepy windowless vans?" I teased. "Mom, in case you've forgotten, I'm in sixth grade and I haven't been abducted a single time."

With a scowl she replied, "Don't even joke about that. It's not funny."

I sighed. "Sorry. I'll be fine. I promise."

I picked up her phone from the counter, stuck it in the back pocket of my jeans, and headed toward the door. "The pass code is 123456," she called out.

"Mom, are you serious?"

"I know. I'm not very creative. Hey, watch out for Casper, okay? He may try to sneak out with you."

I looked around for him, but he was nowhere in sight. He was probably hiding under my bed, wondering how he'd ended up in this strange place. Well, that made two of us.

Things I already miss about Bakersfield

1. *My dad and his ugly blue recliner that he'd never let Mom sell.*

2. *My best friend, Inca, and the way she makes me laugh like nobody else.*

3. *Going to see the peacocks at Hart Park practically anytime I wanted to. You know what you won't find at the beach? Peacocks.*

4. *Mr. Richie and the best school library in the world.*

5. *Meek Pickles at the Haggin Oaks Farmers Market. I mean, where else can you get pickled carrots? They're good, I swear!*

6. *The lines on the doorframe in our old kitchen that show how much Miranda and I have grown every year since we started walking. I saw them every morning as I got myself breakfast.*

7. *This list could be 77 items long if I wanted it to be. So I'll just end with—basically everything.*

Two

Back in third grade, my teacher, Mrs. Arlington, called me "quirky" in my report card. To describe my personality. Mom said quirky isn't bad, it just means I like to do things differently. Like, when Mrs. Arlington gave us an assignment to write a letter to our hero, I wrote to my cat. Everyone else wrote to an athlete or a movie star or to a special family member. In my letter, I made a list of seven reasons why my cat was my hero. For example, when I first wake up, and Casper is asleep at the foot of my bed, he lets me pet his super-soft belly and it's the most comforting thing you could ever imagine.

I like lists; they make me feel good. But if I'd written to a movie star, I would have been lucky to come up with even one thing, much less a whole list.

Sometimes, though, I wonder if I'm too quirky. Or *unusual*—the word Mom uses when she talks about my art and lists. She says it's "unusual" that I love messy art projects as much as I love organizing everything into detailed lists. To me, that's like saying it's unusual if you like both cats *and* dogs. Why not both?

For some reason, I was thinking about that as I walked out the door and down a path that runs across one quiet street before landing at the boardwalk of Mission Beach. It was pretty crowded—lots of people walking, running, and riding bikes. At least our cottage wasn't super close to the amusement park. It's always packed down there. I crossed over into the sand, and as I looked out at the big, blue ocean, the warm sun on my face, I felt a little bit better about life in that moment. Maybe this wouldn't be so bad. Maybe I'd make some new friends right away. Maybe the three of us would get along just fine without Dad around.

Or maybe I was unusual *and* delusional. That was probably it.

I kicked off my flip-flops, picked them up, and walked toward the ocean in the coarse, hot sand. It was a clear March day with hardly a cloud in the sky. I took a deep breath of the salty air and sat down. A few feet ahead of me, closer to the water, a dark-haired girl who looked about my age and a younger boy were making a fancy sand castle with large turrets and a moat around it. The whole thing looked like something you'd see in a sand castle–building contest. I turned and watched a teen girl play Frisbee with her black Lab. She'd throw the Frisbee at him and he'd jump up and catch it. They did it over and over again. It was amazing.

Mom's phone vibrated in my pocket. I pulled it out to see what was happening. It was a text from Dad.

> That child support amount is unacceptable. Come on,
> Wendy. Be reasonable.

I rolled my eyes as I clicked off the screen. *Please. Stop.*

I'd heard them discussing child support on the phone the other night. It didn't make me feel very good that they were arguing about this. About *us*. It reminded me of the time Mom and Dad fought over what kind of vacuum to get when ours broke. Mom wanted an expensive Roomba—the kind that moves around on the floor without anyone pushing it. Dad said he'd always kind of thought that Roombas were for lazy people. Oh my gosh, that made Mom *so* mad. She said they were for *busy* people, not lazy ones, and it was mean of him to call her lazy. He tried to explain that he didn't call *her* lazy, he'd just said what he thought about the Roomba in general. Then they started arguing about *that*.

I felt bad for Mom. And now, I felt bad for my sister and me when they argued about how much money Mom should get for taking care of us.

I was tucking Mom's phone back in my pocket when, out of nowhere, a girl wearing shorts and a polka-dot T-shirt plopped down next to me with a large beach bag. She pulled out two glass bottles and with a smile she asked, "Do you want one of these?"

The polka dots she wore seemed like a good sign—they almost matched the polka dots on my favorite pair of

TOMS—but the bottles, I admit, confused me. They reminded me of the bottles used to serve water at my favorite Italian restaurant back home. I stared at her for a second. She had shoulder-length wavy blond hair, lots of freckles on her nose, and a really friendly smile.

"That's nice of you," I said, "but my bottle collection is out of control right now. So I should probably pass."

She chuckled. "That's funny. And hi. I'm Emma."

"I'm Juliet."

"Are you here on vacation?"

"No. We just moved in to one of the cottages."

"Well, zippity-do-dah," she said in a totally excited, singsongy voice. "You going to the middle school?"

If anyone else had answered that way, it probably would have sounded sarcastic. Mean, even. But all I could hear was happiness in her voice. And I wondered if maybe this girl might be quirky, like me.

I gulped, thinking about her question. Moving had kept me distracted, but it was getting harder and harder to ignore where I'd be in just one short week. "Yeah. Sixth grade."

"Hey, me, too! I live in the tan stucco house with the mint-green trim. On the corner up there?" She pointed behind us, in the general direction. "It's a big house. Because, you know, big family."

"Like, how big?"

"My house or my family?"

"Your family."

"One older sister, two older brothers, and my parents."

I nodded. I felt a little jealous at the mention of the word *parents*.

"So why are you giving away glass bottles, exactly?" I asked.

She set them down in the sand. Her short fingernails were painted light blue. So cute! "You mean it's not totally obvious? Okay, then. I read this book about a boy who put a message in a bottle and threw it in the ocean to see if someone would write him back. I thought to myself, 'I have to try that!'"

Now she really had my attention. "Book? What's the title?"

She shrugged. "I can't remember. I'm really bad at stuff like that—details or whatever. But as soon as I read about it, I wanted to do it, too. Doesn't it sound fun? Like, you can share a secret with someone you've never met before and maybe they'll tell you a secret back. At least, that's what I hope will happen."

"But how will they tell *you* a secret?" I asked. "Wouldn't it be hard to get a bottle back to you?"

"In the book, the boy gave a home address, hoping he'd get a letter. Except my mom said that, for safety reasons, I should just put my email address."

"Oh," I said, feeling kind of silly I didn't think of that. "That makes sense. Do you really think someone will find it and write back, though? What if you're waiting and wondering about it forever?"

She tucked a stray strand of her wavy hair behind her ear. "I guess I don't really know what will happen. All I know is just thinking about the possibilities makes me happy. So I've already won, right?"

I wasn't sure I was hearing her correctly. This girl could be happy just by thinking something *might* happen? I wanted to ask her how that worked, but decided not to. She seemed really focused on wanting to get her note written.

Emma reached into her bag again and pulled out a couple of pads of paper along with two pens. "Write something good, okay?"

"Good?"

"Interesting, I guess. It doesn't have to be a secret, but that's what I'm going to do. It makes it more exciting, I think. Oh, and my mom said it's probably best if we don't give our names. She wants us to be extra careful. Obviously."

I nodded as she handed me the paper and a pen.

Just then, a Frisbee landed right in front of us. We both looked up and saw the dog running over, the girl right behind him, yelling, "Rocky, wait!"

"Sorry," she called out as she came and shooed him away, the Frisbee now in his mouth. "Threw it way too hard that time." She squinted her eyes. "Oh, hi, Emma. Didn't notice that was you."

"Hi, June," Emma said. "No worries."

June stared at the bottles in the sand for just a moment before she turned and ran after Rocky. "See you later!"

"Bye!" Emma called out. She looked at me. "She's in eighth grade. My family has known her family a long time." She gently poked my leg with her pen. "Okay, let's start writing."

I wanted to see what she wrote, but I knew it wasn't really any of my business. If she wanted to share, she would.

The phone in my pocket buzzed again. I decided to ignore it since I didn't want to have to explain everything going on between my parents.

I started on my message.

Dear Stranger,

Hi. I'm J.J. I'm an artist. I draw and paint all the time. My favorite artist is Vincent van Gogh. I love his painting "The Starry Night." And the sunflower one. The seascape one, too. I can't remember the names of those two.

I'll tell you a secret. Sometimes I wish I could live in Vincent's painting of the starry sky. It looks magical. Like every star is different but brilliant and bursting with life and that's exactly how it should be because all together, those stars make up something special.

I wish I could be brilliant and a part of something special.

My email address is artistgirl99@home.com.

Write to me, okay? Unless you're some creepy person, then don't. #nocreepersallowed

Sincerely yours,

J.J.

I read back over my note and wondered if it sounded weird. Maybe. But I decided I didn't care that much. The chances of someone finding it, reading it, and writing me back were probably really small. As long as I made Emma happy, that's what mattered.

She was still working on hers, so I drew a moon surrounded by a bunch of stars at the bottom of my message. When Emma finished writing, she reached into her bag again and pulled out two short pieces of thin, blue ribbon.

"Now roll your letter up, like this," she said as she rolled the piece of paper tightly. "I'll hold it while you tie the ribbon, then we'll switch."

Once we tied the ribbons, we stuck the letters into the bottles. With a black Sharpie we wrote on the outside of the bottles: PLEASE READ THE LETTER INSIDE. Then we swung the attached bottle stoppers into place and sealed them both tightly. Emma stood up and I followed her across the sand. As we passed the girl making the sand castle, she turned and said, "Hi, Emma."

"Hi, Carmen. Nice castle you got there."

"Thanks. My brother loves building them."

We walked away and Emma leaned in and whispered, "That girl is so shy. She hardly ever says a word. I have a couple of classes with her and I don't think I've ever heard her say a whole sentence."

I corrected her. "Until now."

"Right. Until now." She picked up her pace. "Come on. We'll throw them in over here. And then you want to get some ice cream?"

"I didn't bring any money."

"Well, lucky for you, you don't need any."

I gave her a funny look. "How come?"

"My family owns the Frozen Spoon. Free ice cream every day if I want it!"

"But they don't even know me," I said. "Are you sure they won't mind?"

She scoffed. "Trust me, they won't mind. So what do you say?"

"Emma, there's one thing you should know about me," I told her.

"What's that?"

"I love to eat. I will probably never say no to food if you offer it to me. Unless it's something gross like onion-and-broccoli pizza."

She wiggled her eyebrows. "What about onion-and-broccoli ice cream?"

I laughed. "Well, who doesn't love onion-and-broccoli ice cream? Pretty sure it's the best ever."

"Yeah, the best *worst* ever," she said as she laughed along with me.

And just like that, I was feeling a whole lot better about moving to Mission Beach.

My favorite ice cream flavors

1. *Cookie dough, because it's the one time you can eat cookie dough and no one will yell at you, "Don't do that, you might die of salmonella!"*
2. *Mint chocolate chip, because mint combined with chocolate is a magical combination.*
3. *Strawberry, because it's sweet and pink and perfect.*
4. *Rainbow sherbet, because who doesn't love rainbows?*
5. *Vanilla, because sometimes you need a little plain and simple in your life.*

Three

DOUBLE SCOOP

"What'd you do that for?" asked a boy when we turned around to leave the beach. He wore shorts and a T-shirt and a blue Dodgers baseball cap. He and his two friends seemed to be about our age. I guessed they must know Emma.

"Hi, Henry," Emma said in a slightly annoyed tone. "Don't you want to meet my friend Juliet? She just moved here. Juliet, this is Henry, José, and Marcus."

"Hi," I said, my cheeks on fire because I'm not very good at talking to one boy, let alone three. Yikes.

They all kind of mumbled hi or hello and then Henry said, "So? Why'd you do it?"

"Do what?"

"Throw those bottles into the ocean?"

Emma looked at me. I didn't know what to say, so I just shrugged. She turned back to them. "Secret messages. You know, for the mermaids."

"Riiight," Marcus said. "No such thing as mermaids."

"Come on," Henry said. "Be serious. I want to know."

"It doesn't involve sports, so I promise, you wouldn't be interested," Emma said.

"I like things other than sports," Henry said.

"Like what?" Emma said.

"Like video games. And hamburgers. And . . ."

His voice trailed off. I could tell Emma was trying not to laugh.

"Okay, well, we really have to go," she said. "See ya later."

She hurried until she reached the boardwalk, with me following close behind. When we stopped, I turned around to see if they'd followed us, but they were heading toward the ocean.

"Not all the kids at our school are that rude," Emma said. "I promise. I have Henry in P.E. and let's just say he's not the nicest boy in town."

Those two words—*our school*—made me feel like I might throw up. I thought back to P.E. with Inca. When we had the folk dance unit, we had to count off for partners. It didn't matter if you got a boy or a girl, just as long as you had a partner. Inca and I were disappointed when we didn't get to pick each other, but what made it even worse was that I got paired with Maverick, this obnoxious boy who thinks he's the world's greatest athlete. Every time he made a basket during the basketball unit, he'd put his finger high in the air as he ran down the court, like "I'm number one." Every. Single. Time.

Luckily, Inca rescued me from Maverick. She quietly went to our teacher, Mrs. Bennett, and told her Maverick and I had a history of not getting along and would it be all right if she and I were partners instead. It took some convincing on Inca's part, but Mrs. Bennett liked us and so she eventually said okay.

I hoped I wouldn't get stuck with Henry as a dance partner. There's no way I could have that much bad luck in one year, right?

Emma and I both brushed the sand off our feet as best we could before we slipped them into our flip-flops.

"You're probably nervous about starting at a new school, huh?" she said, like she could read my mind.

"Um," I said. "A little." My voice shook as I said it. I laughed. "Okay, a lot."

"Well, don't be. It's a good school, and we're going to have so much fun." She pulled her phone out of her shorts pocket. "Hold on. Just gonna tell Mom we're coming."

I couldn't believe she was talking to me like she'd known me forever. I wondered if she was this way with everyone? Or had she noticed I was alone and felt bad for me? It was a little bit strange and beautiful, all mixed together.

"Do you need to let your mom know, too?" she asked.

"Yeah, I probably should." I texted my sister really quickly and said I'd met a girl my age from my new school and we were going to hang out for a while at her family's ice cream shop.

Miranda replied: Mom says cool! Be home by six, please.

"Okay. This way," Emma said when we'd both finished. We turned right. A family riding bikes zipped around us. "It's just a few blocks."

"Have you lived here your whole life?" I asked.

"Since I was four," she said. "I don't really remember anything else but this place."

"Do both your parents run the shop, or . . . ?"

"My dad is a software consultant and works from home. Well, he travels sometimes, but mostly he works from home. We bought the shop a few years ago, and Mom manages it, but he does some work for it, too. Plus, all of us kids help out in different ways."

"Wow," I said. "So you don't all get sick of each other?"

She laughed again. I loved that she laughed so easily. "I didn't say that. But we're never there all at the same time. It's too small—only a couple of people can work there at a time."

An old man wearing a dingy blue-and-white striped cap, the kind a train conductor might wear, sat on a patio facing the boardwalk. "Hi, Emma," he called as we walked by.

She stopped. "Hi, Mr. Dooney."

"Did you get your message in a bottle sent off?" he asked.

"Yes, sir. This is my friend Juliet. She did one, too."

"I can't wait to hear what happens."

"How long do you think it'll be 'til we hear back?" she asked him.

He took his hat off and rubbed his shiny bald head. "Could be weeks. Could be months. Could be years. Hard to say."

"I hope it's not years," I said. "I'm not that patient."

"Me neither," Emma said. "See you later, Mr. Dooney. We're off to get some ice cream."

"Mmm. Good plan. Enjoy yourselves."

"Bye," we both called.

"He's one of the old-timers in the neighborhood," Emma explained. "He knows just about everybody who lives here. Don't be surprised if he comes to your cottage to welcome you guys to town. What's your family like, anyway?"

Perfect. The question I'd been dreading. I considered giving her some silly answer like "You don't want to know. I live with a bunch of clowns." But it seemed dishonest, in a way. Like I was trying to hide the truth. And even though I'd only known Emma for approximately fifty-three minutes, I liked her. Plus, she'd told me all about her family, so it seemed only fair to be honest and get it all out there.

My friends in Bakersfield had been so understanding when I'd told them what was happening with my parents. I even cried in Inca's room once, when it all got to be too much. Now it was time to start talking about it in a different way, and it was kind of weird. My parents' separation wasn't about to happen, or in the middle of happening. It was basically done. They'd split up, and we'd moved away.

"My mom and dad are separated," I told her. "Probably going to get a divorce. So it's me, my mom, and my fifteen-year-old sister, Miranda."

"I'm sorry," she said. "About your parents, I mean."

"Me, too."

When we got to the little lemon-yellow shop with the words THE FROZEN SPOON painted on a sign in bright blue letters, I smiled. A bell jingled above the door as we walked inside. The place smelled like waffle cones mixed with fresh sea air. Delicious. A mom with two little boys sat at a table, eating ice cream, but there wasn't anyone in line at the counter.

A tall, thin woman with short brown hair, wearing a red-and-yellow apron and a big friendly smile, said, "Hi, girls."

Emma said, "Mom, this is my friend Juliet. She just moved here with her mom and sister."

When she called me her friend, I couldn't have been happier if she'd handed me an empty canvas and a paintbrush.

"That's so great," Emma's mom said as she came around

from behind the counter. "Nice to meet you, Juliet. I'm Joanne. May I ask where you moved from?"

"Bakersfield."

"Ah, not *too* far, then. Have you been to Mission Beach before?"

"Just once, a long time ago. The cottage we're staying in is a rental that belongs to my grandparents. They live up in Carlsbad. Except they're in Europe for a month."

"What does your mom do?"

Like mother, like daughter, I thought. Again I wondered if they did this with everyone they met, or was it just me? I wasn't even sure I knew which one I wanted it to be—that they were super friendly and curious about everyone, or only me? Maybe there just weren't that many new people moving here—like, people who weren't tourists.

"She's a veterinarian," I said. "She starts her new job tomorrow."

"Wonderful," Joanne said. Her eyes turned from me to the customers who were getting up from the table. They threw their garbage in the trash can and walked toward the door. "Have a nice day," Joanne called out.

The woman turned and waved. "Thanks. You, too."

Joanne wiped her forehead with the back of her hand and let out a long breath. "Whew. First time it's been empty since we opened this morning."

Just then, a lanky teen boy came from the back room.

"Mom, I think we might be out of hot fudge. Unless it's hiding somewhere. Or Emma ate all of it."

"Oh, stop," Emma said. She turned to me. "That's my brother Thomas. He's the second oldest." She looked at him. "Be nice, Thomas. I have a new friend here."

"Of course I'll be nice," he said. "What else would I be?"

"Annoying?" Emma said. "Like you usually are?"

"Only when you deserve it," he said.

"Can I get you girls a cone?" Joanne asked. "And then I'll help you find the hot fudge, Thomas. I don't see how we can possibly be out."

"Juliet, you go first. *Be our guest, be our guest*," Emma sang to me, sounding like a star straight out of *Beauty and the Beast*. It made me laugh. "Get a double scoop if you want, right, Mom?"

Joanne walked around to the other side of the freezers and picked up an ice cream scoop. "Absolutely."

"Come on," Emma said, gently pulling on my wrist. "Check out the flavors. This one called lemon pie? It's ah-mazing!"

"Okay," I said. "That sounds good. I'll have that with a scoop of strawberry."

Emma smiled. "Same for me, please! Oh, and, Mom, I'm going to take Emma to our house after this." She looked at me. "If you want to, that is."

"Sure," I said. Because as curious as Emma seemed to be about me, I was just as curious about her. I'd never had a friendship happen this fast before. All of my friends back home I'd met on our cul-de-sac from the time I could ride a tricycle, basically. This was a first for me, and the excitement I felt at already having a new friend? It was shooting-star excitement. Like . . . wow!

To make myself less worried about
moving away from everything I loved,
this is the list I made of things I
could do at the beach.

1. Visit the bookmobile that Grandma said is nearby.
2. Build a unique creation out of sand (I'm thinking a sea turtle).
3. Fly a kite on a windy day.
4. Buy saltwater taffy and eat it while walking on the beach.
5. Watch the sun set.
6. Roast marshmallows over a bonfire.
7. Ride my bike the entire length of the boardwalk.
8. ~~Maybe find someone to hang out with so I don't have to do these things alone.~~

Four

NEW FRIEND

"This is it," Emma said as we approached a door on the second floor. "My room."

It was painted mint green and had a bunk bed, a dresser, and a bookcase filled with books. Lots of books. There were clothes scattered on the floor, and she quickly went to work picking them up. I glanced around at her walls. A few shiny gold trophies sat on a single shelf, and she had posters of cute animals—hedgehogs and foxes mostly.

"What are the trophies for?" I asked.

"I play soccer," she said. "What about you?"

"I did gymnastics for a while," I said. "Didn't last long, though."

Back then, Dad would take me to the gym every Saturday morning. Afterward, we'd stop at a café where I'd get a hot chocolate and a cinnamon roll and he'd get a coffee and a muffin. I liked that part a lot more than I liked the time at the gym.

"How come?" she asked.

"How come what?"

"How come it didn't last long?"

"I didn't feel like I was good enough. I wish I'd been able to do it without looking around and comparing myself to everyone else. Mom told me I should do it because it's fun. And I wanted to. But it's not that easy, you know?"

"Yeah," she said. "I get that. Gymnastics seems really hard, too. I love watching it during the Olympics."

"Same."

She reached for a tin of mints on the nightstand by her bed. "I have a thing about fresh breath."

"Hey, me, too! But my favorites are Tic Tacs. I've loved them forever. They're my dad's favorite, too."

She popped a mint into her mouth and passed them to me. After I took one, I placed the tin back in its place and went over to her bookcase. There were a bunch of books I'd never heard of.

"Have you been to the bookmobile yet?" she asked.

"No. My grandma told me about it, though. I want to go."

"We should go together," she said. "You'll love it. If you love books, that is."

"I totally do." I turned around. "Is it open now?"

"No, not on Sundays. Tomorrow, I have to help out in the shop for a little while in the morning. And then I have plans with my friend Shelby after that. But Tuesday I could go with you, if you want?"

For some reason, when she mentioned Shelby, I felt an icy-cold prickle shoot through my body. It was ridiculous. What did I expect—that Emma, who had lived here most of her life, wouldn't have any friends? Of course she had friends. She was sweet and fun and, okay, very curious, and I shouldn't be surprised if she had fifty friends. She seemed to know just about everyone in the neighborhood; I'd seen that myself. But I didn't have anyone else here, and so it hurt, thinking of her off having fun while I'd be sitting at home, alone.

All of a sudden, I felt so homesick for Bakersfield, my stomach hurt. "I should probably get home," I told Emma.

"Already? But we just got here."

"I know. Sorry. My mom didn't want me to stay long, though. We still, um, have lots of unpacking to do and stuff."

"Oh, yeah. Right. Okay, well, I'll walk you out."

I followed her down the stairs and watched as her sister bounded through the front door. At least, I assumed it was her sister.

"Juliet, this is Molly. Molly, Juliet. She's new to my school, starting next week."

"Hey," Molly said as she took off her pink Ray-Bans and threw them onto the entryway table along with her keys. "Is Dad home? I need to ask him something."

The squeeze on my stomach got tighter. If I wanted to ask my dad something, I'd have to call him. Or email him. They were so lucky. And they probably didn't even know it.

"Yeah," Emma said. "In his office."

Outside, on the front porch, Emma reached her arms out and pulled me into a hug. Suddenly, I was sure I had met someone special. She had been curious because she cared. Which was the best kind of curiosity, really. And it's not like it was her fault that she had a big family while mine was small and broken.

"Okay, cross your fingers someone will read our bottle messages and reply," she said as I turned to go down the steps. "And that it won't take three years."

"I will. It'll probably be a mermaid," I teased, turning back to see her face because I knew it'd make her smile. And it did.

"Yeah, probably." She started singing, *"Under the sea—"*

"Under the sea," I piped in.

"Do you remember how many blocks to go before your street?" Emma asked me.

"Four? I think? I know the street name, though, so I'll find it."

"Oh!" she said. "Hold on. Let me give you my phone number so we can do something Tuesday."

I pulled out Mom's phone and put her number in as she told it to me. So we wouldn't see each other tomorrow, but I could wait until Tuesday. Maybe. Somehow.

"Call me Tuesday morning," Emma said. "The book-mobile opens at nine."

"Okay." I waved. "See you later. Thanks for the ice cream!"

"Like my dad always says, there's more where that came from. Bye!"

Once I'd gone a little way, I pulled out the phone and checked the time. It was a few minutes after four. I had more than forty hours to wait until Tuesday morning. Forty hours may have well been forty days—it seemed so far away and I had no idea what I'd do with myself until then. Still, things could have been worse. I could have not met Emma at all.

My favorite things to paint

* *The night sky*
* *Flowers*
* *Owls*
* *Cats*
* *Trees*
* *Cupcakes*

Five

QUICK RESPONSE

Monday morning, Mom left early for her new job. When I got up, Miranda was gone, too. She'd told us over dinner the night before that she planned on spending most of the break in the ocean or at the nearby pool, training. Training for what, you ask? Well, for some reason, my sister has dreamt of being a lifeguard since she was five years old. And moving to Mission Beach gave her a great opportunity—to try out for the Junior Lifeguard program with the city of San Diego.

Tryouts were coming up in May and she'd told us that in order to compete with other people who had been in the program before, she was going to have to work really, really hard to get in shape.

So with both of them doing their thing, I decided to make Monday an art day. In the morning, I sketched pictures with pencils in my drawing pad. After a couple of hours of that, I got my paints ready so I could spend the afternoon working at my easel. My mom and dad gave me the easel for Christmas last year. It's a small one that sits on my desk so it doesn't take up a lot of room.

In between drawing and painting, I made my favorite lunch: a turkey sandwich with lots of pickles. Maybe I should call it a pickle sandwich with a little bit of turkey, which is much more accurate. As I was eating my most delicious sandwich, the phone rang. Mom can't imagine a world without a real phone in the house, so our landline had been set up as soon as we moved in.

"Hello?"

"Hey, Pooh, it's me." Miranda. Yes, we call each other Pooh sometimes.

"You coming home for lunch?" I asked.

"No, I met a couple of girls who are training for the tryouts, too. We're gonna hang out here, at the beach. Probably get some tacos. Thought I should check in with you, though, and make sure you're doing okay."

"I'm fine. I guess."

"What does that mean?"

I sighed. *It means I'm here by myself, in a new place, with my friends and my dad hours away, and I'm trying my best to forget all that.*

But all I said was, "Nothing."

"What are you doing?"

"Eating a sandwich. Then I'm going to paint."

"Good. I gotta go. I'll see you later, okay?"

"Okay. Oh, hey, Miranda, do we have Internet?"

"Yeah. The house had it before we moved in."

"All right. Thanks. Bye."

"Bye."

I took my sandwich over to the desk where Mom had set up the desktop computer. I watched a Bob Ross painting video for a few minutes and then switched over to check my email. I had a message from Inca, but I didn't open it because I was too excited about another message. The subject line said: "I found your bottle."

My first thought was: WHAT!?!? My second thought was: No way!

I clicked on the message and started reading.

Hi, J.J.,

I got your message. You know, the message you sent out to sea in a bottle?

You're not going to believe it. I love Vincent van Gogh's paintings, too! The seascape one is called "Seascape near Les Saintes-Maries-de-la-Mer." I think it's my favorite, if I had to choose one.

Do you really want to be a part of something special? Because I have an idea.

I wish on stars all the time. I bet you do, too. And I was thinking about all of the other people like us. Sometimes their wishes come true, but sometimes they don't. Maybe the stars need helpers now and then. So let's help! Maybe we could call ourselves the Starry Beach Club (since the Starry Night Club sounds like a place where old people go to dance). Whatever we call it, we'll make Vincent proud.

But first, you have to prove to me you can do it. Show me that you are clever, creative, sneaky, and diligent. Find someone's wish. Make it come true. Then email me and tell me about it.

Sincerely Yours,

Some Kid at the Beach

Starry Beach Club Member #1

I read the email three times. I checked the address to see if it gave me any clues as to who might have written it, but it was from somekidatthebeach@home.com. Yeah, no help there at all.

I wanted to call Emma and tell her about it. I couldn't, though. She was hanging out with Shelby, and she'd specifically told me to call her Tuesday morning.

There was nothing to do but wait.

Some ways I might be clever

* *When I want to cuddle and my cat doesn't feel like it, I make a tuna fish sandwich with lots of pickles and share a teensy bit with him (the tuna, not the pickles).*
* *On the nights I really don't want to do the dishes, I make sure I have a lot of homework saved up.*
* *I love getting mail, so I write letters to my grandma and she writes me back.*
* *I don't like onions, so when something has onions in it, I tell my brain they're actually white pickles.*
* *I save the boring stuff to read for the nights when I can't fall asleep.*

(I feel like this is a really lame list, but it's all I've got.)

Six

HI, DAD

Mom didn't get home until almost seven. I was starving. Miranda had gotten home around three. I almost told her about the email from Some Kid but decided not to. She probably would have said it was a stupid joke and told me to ignore it. Or she would have told me I better not email the person back in case it was an Internet predator. Except what kind of Internet predator wants to make people's wishes come true? And besides, as long as I didn't give them any personal information, how would Some Kid know anything about me? I could be an eighty-nine-year-old hippie yoga instructor, or a tourist who'd already gone back to a fancy apartment in Manhattan.

Since Mom was tired from a long first day, we had canned tomato soup and grilled cheese sandwiches for dinner. Yum. Once Miranda stopped talking about her new friends, I jumped in to ask about plans for the next day.

"Mom, Emma invited me to go to the bookmobile with her tomorrow. Is that okay?"

My mother put her elbows on the table and rubbed her temples. "I suppose. Just please, stick together. You said her parents are generally around, right?"

"Yes."

"All right. But don't make a nuisance of yourself. I'm sure they have their hands full with four children."

"I won't."

Mom's phone rang. She glanced at the number, leaned back, and pushed the phone toward me. "Want to talk to your father? I'm not really up for it right now."

She got up with her dishes and went toward the kitchen while I picked up the phone.

"Hi, Dad. It's Juliet."

"Oh. Hi. Your mom busy?"

"Kind of. Yeah."

"I see. So, how are you? You girls settled into the new place yet?"

"Mostly. There's still some boxes of stuff Mom doesn't know what to do with."

"Yeah. Moving's a big job. Think you're gonna like it, though? Eventually?"

I wanted to say, "What does it matter? You didn't give me a choice about any of this." But I didn't. I said, "I hope so."

"I bet you will. It's a wonderful place. Hey, I ran into Inca at the grocery store yesterday. She said to tell you hello. I think she said she'd email you, too."

"Yeah. I read it earlier and replied."

"Okay, good."

It got quiet. Were we really out of things to talk about that fast? It made me realize how different this was going to be. When Dad and I were together, eating cinnamon rolls or going for nature hikes or even just watching *The Great British Bake Off*, it didn't matter if we didn't talk. Now we were supposed to *just* talk and it wasn't supposed to matter if we weren't together. But it did matter. To me, anyway.

When I couldn't think of anything else to say, I asked, "You want to say hi to Miranda?"

"Sure."

"Okay. Bye, Dad."

"Good talking to you. See you in a few weeks, okay?"

"Yeah."

After I scooted the phone over to Miranda, I picked up my dishes and went into the kitchen. Mom was at the sink, washing the pans by hand.

"Everything all right?" I asked as I put my dishes in the dishwasher.

"Yes," Mom said. "Just tired. Think I'll finish up here and go soak in the tub."

"It's really tiny."

She looked at me funny. "What?"

"The tub. It's not like the one we had at home."

The confused look disappeared, and in its place was sadness. "Oh. Right. I forgot. Well, guess I'll go to bed and read for a while, then."

She rinsed off the pans and put them on the drying rack. As she walked past me, she said, "You girls are good, right?"

Did she mean right now, this minute? Or just in general? Either way, I knew there was really only one way to answer. "Yeah. We're fine."

She smiled slightly. "Good night, Juju Bean."

"Night."

As she left the kitchen, I heard Miranda tell her, "He wants you to call him tomorrow."

"We'll see," she said. "Good night."

I sat down across from my sister. After I heard Mom shut the bathroom door, I said, "Maybe he misses her. Maybe that's why he called."

"I doubt it."

"I wish there was something we could do," I said.

"About what?"

"About them. Mom and Dad. Get them to see that they're better together than apart."

She stood up and gathered her dinner dishes. "I think they've made up their minds. It's just going to be hard for a while, Pooh. For all of us."

I put my chin in my hands and sighed. "Want to help me set up the DVD player and watch a movie?"

"No," Miranda called from the kitchen. "I have plans to play a game online with a friend."

She went to her room and I sat there alone for a minute before I remembered that in my email I'd asked Inca if she wanted to Skype later. I checked my inbox, but she hadn't responded. Since I was there, I read Some Kid's note again. And then I printed it out. Because no way would Emma believe it unless she saw it for herself.

After it printed, I heard Miranda mutter something to herself about her dinosaur of a laptop. Mom came out of the bathroom and gave me a little wave before she went into her bedroom. The cottage was super tiny, so my mom and sister weren't far. I mean, they were so close I could practically hear them breathing. Still, it felt like that giant ocean outside our door was actually inside the house—me on one side and them on the other.

I thought of Dad, back home, probably feeling the same way. I opened my email and started typing.

Hi Dad,

Sorry I didn't talk to you very long when you called earlier. I'm not really used to talking to you on the phone. And all of this is just really different. I miss you. I miss my friends. I even miss the sound of cars driving by outside my window. I know a lot of people love the sound of waves, but I'm not used to it. I'm not used to any of this. Since you're probably not used to living by yourself either, I bet you understand.

Guess I'll go to bed now. It's early, but I can read a book. Then I'll try to fall asleep listening to those waves. Maybe someday I'll like that sound like everyone else. Not tonight, though. Tonight, all they do is make me miss the sound of the cars even more.

There's something I've always remembered from when I took swimming lessons. On the first day, when I was holding on to you because I didn't want to go to the teacher, you told me that every time I got in the pool, I'd feel a little less afraid. You told me that I just had to get the hardest part out of the way first. Maybe right now, we're getting the hardest part out of the way. Which means, things can only get better. I hope so.

Love you!

Juliet

Boredom is

* *not fun.*
* *kind of sad.*
* *the opposite of exciting.*
* *a weird word.*
* *very boring!*

Seven

SAFE PLACE

I called Emma the next morning and we agreed to meet near Mr. Dooney's house at nine, since it was about halfway between hers and mine. I stuck the printed email in my pocket, along with my Tic Tacs to share, and headed out.

When Emma saw me walking toward her, she waved and looked like she was truly happy to see me.

"I have to tell you something," she said when we met up.

"Me, too." I reached into my pocket and fished out the mints. I took one and then offered one to her.

"Thanks," she said. "You go first. I can wait."

I couldn't help but wonder if she'd gotten an email, too. I guess I'd soon find out. I put the Tic Tacs back and pulled out the printed email. "I already heard back."

She gave me a funny look. "Heard back?"

"Yes. Someone found my message in a bottle and wrote to me."

Her mouth opened wide as her hands grabbed my arms.

"No way! Already?" She looked at the piece of paper in my hand. "Is that it? The email you got back?"

"Yes."

She reached for it. "Can I see it? Please?"

I smiled. "That's why I brought it." She grabbed hold of it, but I didn't let go. "Before you read it, there's something you should know, or it won't make sense."

"What?"

"In my note, I talked about my favorite painting, *The Starry Night*. I know this might sound weird, but . . ." I paused, wondering if I should say more. It was one thing to tell a stranger what I'd said in my letter. But tell Emma? I didn't want to do anything to mess up this new friendship. Her green eyes stared at me, full of questions, but I saw something else there, too. I saw a safe place. She would understand. I knew it as sure as I knew a cinnamon roll with hot chocolate is the best breakfast in the entire world.

So I said, "I talked about how I sometimes wish I could live in that magical painting. That I want to be brilliant, like the stars he painted, and feel like I'm a part of something special."

"Wow," she whispered, like I'd just told her a very important secret and she really appreciated that. "When I said make it good, you really went for it."

I let go of the message and nervously pulled on the strings of my hoodie. "Once I started writing, it all just kind of . . . came out. I don't know. I can't explain it. Anyway, wait until you see the reply. You won't believe it."

She fanned the piece of paper in front of her face. "I think I need to sit down for this." So we headed for the beach and plopped down on the sand. It was a cloudy day and kind of chilly. I zipped my hoodie up all the way.

You know how it feels when you get your report card in the mail and your mom makes you sit there while she opens it and reads it? That's kind of how I felt as I waited for Emma to read the letter. When she finished, she looked at me and said, "The Starry Beach Club? Is she for real?"

"Sounds like it to me."

She stood up and started pacing.

"When did you get the email?" she asked.

"Yesterday afternoon. It must have washed ashore really soon after we left on Sunday."

"Or someone saw us throw the bottles in and went out and grabbed one before it went too far." She stopped and looked at me. "I know! I bet it was Henry and his friends."

I shook my head. "No way."

"Why not?"

"Because they wouldn't have known the name of the seascape painting. And can you even see one of them using the word 'diligent'?"

"No, but they could have looked it up," she replied. "Or maybe they had help writing the email. Like an older sister

49

or something. Because, remember, they really wanted to know what we were up to."

"Emma, I just don't think so. Besides, I don't *want* it to be one of them."

"Wait!" she said, sticking her finger in the air. "I've got it! Did you see how June stared at the bottles before she ran off? She was curious. And this note *sounds* like someone older than us, doesn't it?"

"Uh, I'm not sure," I said. "But there were a lot of people on the beach yesterday. And we threw those bottles so hard. It couldn't have just come right back from where I threw it."

She nodded slowly as she stared out at the ocean, like she was lost deep in thought. I stayed quiet until she turned to me and said, "We could guess and guess and guess, and there'd be no way to find out for sure. So you know what this means?"

"What?"

"We need to try and do what this person says. And then, hopefully . . ."

"Hopefully, we'll get to meet member number one of the Starry Beach Club?"

Emma grinned. "Exactly."

Some other words for "diligent"

(thanks to the thesaurus)

* *Persistent*
* *Careful*
* *Tireless*
* *Eager*
* *Conscientious*

*(*Quirky *or* different *is not a synonym for* diligent. *I'm worried.)*

Eight

MRS. BUTTON

"So we need to find someone to help?" Emma asked as we made our way down the boardwalk. A seagull flew past us, headed toward the ocean. "Like what? Help an old woman at the grocery store with her bags of groceries?"

"Are we going to be Girl Scouts or wish makers?" I teased. "I'm thinking it should probably be something bigger. Much bigger."

I thought about telling her I was worried I might not be all of the things Some Kid wanted me to be. Okay, creative, yes. But the rest? Clever? Diligent? What if I wasn't the type of person the kid had in mind for their club? But I decided not to say anything for now.

Emma seemed to be thinking out loud. "Whatever it is, it should be something where we can be clever, sneaky, and creative. But how do we find something like that?"

"I have no idea," I said. "Just keep a lookout?"

She giggled. "That sounds like a pirate. *Ahoy, matey, go*

to the bow and keep a lookout. Hey, maybe it should be a pirate club instead."

"But the Starry Beach Club sounds so much more mature," I teased.

"Sophisticated," she said.

"Exactly."

We walked for a little while in silence. That's when I remembered she'd wanted to tell me something.

"Hey, what was it you wanted to tell me earlier?"

"Oh! I almost forgot. I asked my mom if you could sleep over tonight. And she said yes." She turned to me. "That is, if you want to. I just thought, since it's spring break, why not?"

I grinned. "I'd love to! I'll call my mom later and ask her."

"Okay. Cool." She pointed up ahead, to the parking lot of a grocery store, where the bookmobile was parked. "There it is!"

"Wow. I love it." Up close, the bookmobile was much prettier than I'd imagined. It had a mural painted on the side with the beach and the ocean and a boy sitting next to a giant sand castle, reading a book. And in big, blue letters it said BOOKMOBILE BY THE BEACH.

"I know, right? Mr. and Mrs. Button let tourists use it and any of us locals who want to use it, too, even though there's a library not too far. It's just so cute, I like coming here instead."

"Mr. and Mrs. Button? What a sweet name."

Emma smiled. "Wait until you meet them. They are super sweet, trust me."

We walked up the steps and into the open door of the bookmobile.

"Hello, Mrs. Button," Emma called.

There was a small wooden counter directly in front of the entrance. To the left of us were two long rows of wooden bookshelves, packed with books. It really did feel like a teensy-tiny library. On wheels!

A short, round woman stood at one of the shelves, her back turned to us. When Emma spoke, she spun around and smiled. She had on a red T-shirt with big black letters that said READ.

"Emma!" Mrs. Button said as she slipped her reading glasses off and stuck them on top of her head. "How nice to see you. And you've brought a friend."

"This is Juliet. She just moved here from Bakersfield."

"How wonderful," Mrs. Button said. "Nice to meet you, Juliet. I won't ask you if there's a Romeo in your life. You are far too young for that."

I get comments like that about my name sometimes. I guess when there is a world-famous Shakespeare play titled *Romeo and Juliet*, it's gonna happen.

"Isn't it interesting that both of you have names from literary masterpieces?" she continued. "*Emma* is the title of a book by Jane Austen. Oh, I do love Jane Austen. *Pride and*

Prejudice is my favorite book of hers. It helped me through a particularly difficult time in my life. I will always be so very thankful to dear Jane. Her words were like a salve to my soul—exactly what I needed when I was feeling blue."

"Like chicken soup for your feelings?" I asked. As soon as I said it, I wanted to take it back. It seemed like a very strange—or *quirky*—thing to say.

But Mrs. Button's eyes got big and round, just like a pair of shiny brown buttons. "Yes, Juliet, that is exactly right! Oh, I love that so much. May I write that down in my notebook of beautiful things?"

Loved it? Wow, maybe Mrs. Button was quirky just like me. "Sure!" I told her.

She scurried over to her tiny desk and picked up a brown leather journal and a pen and scribbled the words down. As she did that, Emma leaned in and whispered, "She loves writing in her notebook of beautiful things."

It made me feel good that Mrs. Button had chosen something I'd said to put in that elegant notebook of hers. It also made me curious. What other kinds of beautiful things were on those pages? I was dying to know. But it was probably like a diary, in a way, and not really any of my business.

"Oh, that's so lovely," Mrs. Button said. "Thank you, Juliet. Now please, don't let me keep you from browsing for books. If you need help with anything, just ask. That's what I'm here for."

"Do I need to fill out paperwork to get a card or anything?" I asked.

"Yes, indeed," she said. "It's a simple form. Would you like to do it now or wait until you find some books?"

"I can do it now."

She pulled out a clipboard with a form attached and a pen. I stepped over to the counter and put my name at the top of the form: Juliet Kelley.

"Uh-oh," I said. "I don't have my address memorized."

"Just put the street name, that's fine. The phone number is the most important. So we know how to get ahold of you if we need to."

I wrote the street name and my mom's cell number, since I did have that memorized, and signed the bottom. Super easy.

Then Mrs. Button handed me a paper card and said, "We do things the old-fashioned way here. Write your name on the bottom. Then when you find what books you want to borrow, bring them to me and I'll check them out for you. You are allowed three books at any given time. For locals, like you and Emma, books are due in three weeks. Any questions?"

"I don't think so," I said.

When she smiled, the lines near her eyes crinkled. "Okay, then. I hope you find something wonderful to read."

"Where's Mr. Button?" Emma asked.

"He's hoping to come by this afternoon for a bit," Mrs. Button replied. "He hasn't been feeling well."

"Oh," Emma said, sounding disappointed. "I hope he's all right."

"Thank you, Emma. He'll be sad that he missed you."

Just then, a teen girl stepped inside. Mrs. Button turned to greet her, and as she did, Emma and I stepped back to the shelves to look at books.

"I'm going to see if they have any books about Vincent van Gogh," I whispered. "I want to learn more about him."

Emma smiled. "Good idea. I think I'm going to see if they have any books about pirates. See if I can get some lookout tips."

Reasons I love reading books

1. *It's fun! Okay, but why is it fun?*
2. *Books take you to faraway places.*
3. *Reading a story is like watching a movie in your brain.*
4. *Maybe you can't be a wizard or a time traveler in real life, but you can imagine what it feels like while you're reading.*
5. *When I'm feeling nervous, a good book helps me feel better.*
6. *When I'm feeling sad, a good book helps me feel better.*
7. *Even if a book makes me sad, I don't mind because I'm sharing my sadness with someone in the story.*
8. *A book can be sneaky, teaching you things without you knowing it.*
9. *A character struggling with the same problems you're struggling with can make you feel a little less alone in the world.*
10. *I guess it's really true—a good book is like chicken soup for your feelings!*

Nine

JUST PEACHY

Emma and I each found three books to read, including one I checked out called *Vincent van Gogh: Portrait of an Artist*. We chatted about our favorite books and music and other fun stuff on the way back to her house. When we got there, the brother I hadn't met yet was sweeping the porch. I couldn't help noticing how he had muscles the size of mountains. Or big hills, anyway.

"This is Lance," Emma said as we walked past him.

"Hi," I said. "I'm Juliet."

"Hey" was all he said.

Inside, Thomas was vacuuming the front room.

Emma motioned for me to follow her upstairs. When we got away from the noise of the vacuum, I asked, "Do you all have to do morning chores?"

"We don't *have* to," she said. "But Mom makes a list every day of things that need to be done around the house.

And everyone is supposed to pick one or two things off the list. Mom calls it the Step Up and Do It System. If you step up and do something from the list, you get to write your name on a slip of paper and stick it in the jar. Every Friday, Mom draws a name from the jar, and the person whose name is chosen wins a thirty-dollar appreciation jackpot. So basically, the more you work, the better your chances."

"That's super creative. Maybe your mom should join our club."

Emma laughed. "Um, no. And let's just keep this whole thing to ourselves for now, okay? I like having something none of them know about for a change. Something that's all mine." She gave my arm a squeeze. "Or all ours, I should say. You know what I mean?"

"I think so."

It was probably hard being the youngest in a big family. Maybe that's why writing a secret message in a bottle had interested her so much.

We went into Emma's room and sat on the floor. I set my three books down next to me and started flipping through the one about Vincent.

"I figure you and I can make dinner tonight," Emma said before she broke into song. *"On top of spaghetti . . ."* She smiled. "My favorite. And it'll be pretty easy with Mom's sauce that's defrosting in the fridge."

"Then you can put your name in for the jackpot?"

"Yep. Even though I won last week's jackpot, so if I win again so soon, my brothers and sister are going to be really mad. Which is exactly why I want to try and win. Hey, when do you want to ask your mom about sleeping over?"

"Can I text her with your phone?"

"Sure." As she reached for her phone, I stopped flipping pages when I reached a chapter called "Vincent and Friends."

"Do you think the person who emailed me *really* likes Vincent van Gogh's artwork?" I asked Emma.

"Probably. Why would they say so if they didn't?"

"I don't know. It's like—what are the chances of that being true?"

"What are you worried about, exactly?"

"I'm not worried. I'm . . . what's the word when you feel like something's too good to be true?"

"Uh, I don't know." She started tapping on the keyboard of her phone.

"What are you doing?"

"Asking Lance. He'll know."

It only took a few seconds before a message buzzed back. Emma read it and then said, "You're skeptical?"

"That's it! I'm skeptical."

She handed the phone to me so I could text my mom.

"Well, were you skeptical about moving here and making friends?" Emma asked.

I finished my message and put the phone down between us. "Um . . . yes."

"And how'd that work out?"

I laughed. "So far, so good."

"My dad always says, 'Believe in the good. It's a lot more fun than believing in the bad.'"

I must have not looked convinced, because she continued, "Maybe Some Kid had been thinking about doing something like this for a long time, and then you gave them the push they needed to get started. Plus an awesome name for the club."

I ran my finger down the side of the book as I thought about it. "Hm. Maybe."

"You know what else I think?" Emma asked.

"What?"

"Maybe you shouldn't worry about who the person is for now. It makes for a better story, you know? Girl throws a bottle into the ocean with a note that says how much she loves a famous painting. Some Kid answers back, says here's what you do to join a secret club named after that famous painting. Girl does what she says and *becomes a member of the club!* See what I mean?"

I shifted onto my knees. "But I'm so curious who it is, and if she—"

Emma interrupted me. "Or he."

I groaned. "Or he, is really and truly a fan of Vincent like I am. Because I just . . . I hate being lied to."

I don't know why I said that. It sort of slipped out accidentally. Like a drop of ketchup slipping off the end of a hot dog. I hoped with every inch of my heart Emma wouldn't ask me about it. She was a curious person and she'd probably be *really* curious about what I meant, but I didn't want to talk about it. Maybe someday I'd feel like telling her why I hated lies so badly. Not today, though. I stared at the book, avoiding Emma's eyes, and counting in my head, wishing the moment away. *One. Two. Three.*

Emma shrugged and didn't look at me suspiciously or anything. "I think we have to wait and see, as hard as it is. You know, Some Kid might not even live around here." She reached for the mints on her nightstand. "They could live across the bay or in San Francisco, even."

I felt my shoulders drop with relief. Could she tell I hadn't wanted to talk about the lying? Maybe, maybe not. Either way, she was a good friend. That I knew for sure.

"I don't think so," I said as I accepted the mints and popped one into my palm. "The bottle didn't have time to go that far."

"Juliet?"

"Yeah?"

"There's no way to know if they're lying to us," she said in almost a whisper. "All we can do is hope for the best. Do you *want* to believe they're being honest?"

Here's the thing about Emma. When she talks to you? It's like a soft, warm blanket talking to you, because all you want to do is wrap yourself up in it. Soothing.

"Yes," I said.

"Me, too. So I say, let's believe."

Sometimes a comforting, warm blanket is exactly what you need. "Okay. Sorry to be so paranoid or whatever."

She smiled. "It's fine. It's not like you get an email every day asking to be a member of a very secret club."

When the phone buzzed a moment later, Emma reached for it. "It's your mom. She says: 'Sounds good. Have fun!'"

Someone knocked on the door.

"Come in," Emma called out.

The door opened and Mr. Muscle, I mean, Lance, stood there, grinning sheepishly. "Emma," he said. "You didn't answer back when I texted you. Can you please come help me with the pie? You're the best at rolling out the crust."

"No," she said. "If I do it, how are you going to get better at it?"

"But that's the thing; I'm never gonna get better at it," he said. "It's beyond me. I've tried. You know I've tried."

She looked at me. "Lance loves to eat, but he always wants the rest of us to do the work."

"That isn't true," he said. He put his hands together and pleaded. "It'll take you five minutes. Ten, tops. I already made the dough. I just need you to work your magic and get it in the pie plate."

Emma sighed. "What kind are you making?"

"Peach. With some of the peaches Mom canned last

summer. It'll be so good. You know you want some. I already told Mom to bring home some vanilla bean to go with it."

"Do you like peach pie?" Emma asked me.

"I'd say it's my second favorite."

She leaned forward. "You any good at rolling out the crust?"

"Uh, I've never baked a pie before," I said. "My mom says that's what grocery store bakeries are for."

Emma hopped up, unzipped her hoodie, and threw it on the floor. "All right, you win, Lance. Only because Juliet's having dinner with us tonight and she totally deserves some homemade pie."

"Awesome," Lance said. He looked at me as I got to my feet. "You should come around more often, Juliet. You're a good influence on my sister."

Emma gave Lance a slight shove as she walked by him. "Yeah. You got lucky this time."

We went downstairs and I watched as she rolled out the bottom crust. "The key is to use lots of flour," she told Lance and me.

For the top crust, I helped her cut the dough into strips, which she crisscrossed over the mound of peaches.

"It looks *so* good," I said when it was finished.

"That's for sure," Lance said as he picked up the pie and slipped it into the oven. "Nice work."

"You're welcome," Emma said as she poked her brother in the chest.

"Thanks. You're the best sister ever," he said in a very sarcastic voice.

Emma turned to me. "Aren't you glad you don't have brothers?"

But all I could do was shrug. So far, having a big family looked pretty great to me.

Reasons I hate lying

1. Because the most horrible lie was told to me once
    and I will never, ever forget how it feels.

I can't even think of any more reasons because thinking about
reason #1 makes me so upset.

Ten

SAD MEMORIES

I can't remember how old I was, exactly. Six or seven, I think. The four of us, Mom, Dad, Miranda, and I, were all at the kitchen table, eating dinner. Dad had said to Mom, "Wendy, did you hear that Bill and Connie are getting a divorce?"

"Oh, no," Mom said. "I'm so sorry to hear that."

"Bill and Connie?" Miranda asked. "You mean, Jordan's parents?"

Mom nodded.

I don't really remember Jordan the way Miranda does. Jordan babysat us when we were younger. I had a bigger question on my mind, anyway.

"What's a divorce?" I asked.

"It's when two married people decide to stop living together," Mom explained.

"Why?" I asked.

"Usually because they don't love each other anymore,"

Dad said. "But there can be other reasons, too. It's something you'll understand better when you're older."

I didn't want to wait to understand, though. I wanted to know right then. Because it didn't make any sense to me—how you could just stop loving someone? I'd never stop loving my family, I thought. I might get angry at them. But I'd still *love* them even if I didn't like them very much for a little while.

"Would *you* ever get a divorce?" I asked.

"No," Dad said.

Mom kind of laughed. "We probably couldn't afford it."

And then one of them changed the subject and that was the end of that.

But I didn't forget. When they sat Miranda and me down one rainy Sunday afternoon in February, the two of us on the love seat and the two of them on either end of the sofa, and told us they had decided to separate, it was the first thing I thought of.

"But you said you wouldn't," I told them. "When Jordan's parents divorced, you said that wouldn't happen to us."

Dad rubbed his face with his hands before he stared at me, looking kind of stunned. "Wow. You remember that conversation, Juliet?"

"Yes," I said. "Probably because I was so shocked that a family could stop loving each other."

"Not a family, honey," Mom said. "Two married people. There's a difference."

I didn't get how Mom could sit there so calmly. Like she was telling us what chores we needed to do instead of how our family was never going to be the same again. I glanced over at Miranda next to me, but I think she was sort of in shock or something. She just sat there, her mouth open slightly and her forehead all wrinkly.

Mom continued, "Things change sometimes, Juju Bean. There are never any guarantees in life. About anything."

I don't think I really understood what she meant. So I kept pushing. "But I asked if it would ever happen to you guys, and Dad said no."

Maybe he hadn't said, "I promise," but it felt like a broken promise—a *lie*—all the same. A special, invisible promise I'd tucked into a pocket of my heart that was suddenly shattered.

"We want the two of you to know we love you very much," Dad said. "And that the love we have for you will not change because of this decision."

"Did we do something wrong?" I asked.

"No, honey," Mom said. Her eyes filled with tears. "You didn't do anything. This isn't about you. Please believe that."

By then, Miranda was crying, too. "Who will we live with?" she asked. "What happens next?"

And so they told us all the gory details. They were putting the house up for sale. Dad was going to move into a three-bedroom apartment, with enough space for Miranda and me to visit. We would live with Mom most of the time, at Grandma and Grandpa's beach house in San Diego.

"Why?" I asked as the tears I'd fought back finally won.

Mom got up from her spot, kneeled down in front of me, took me in her arms, and held me while I sobbed.

"Why?" I asked over and over again. "Please tell me. Why?"

"You're too young to understand," she whispered. "It's what we have to do."

But we didn't *have* to. It felt like another lie. And as I ran upstairs to my room, slamming the door behind me before I fell onto my bed, I wondered if my entire life had just been one big, fat lie.

My favorite sad books

(because sometimes you want to cry for someone besides yourself)

* *Bridge to Terabithia* by Katherine Paterson
* *The One and Only Ivan* by Katherine Applegate
* *Little Women* by Louisa May Alcott
* *Where the Red Fern Grows* by Wilson Rawls
* *One for the Murphys* by Lynda Mullaly Hunt
* *Charlotte's Web* by E. B. White

Eleven

WISH FOUND

As Emma and I headed to my house to get an overnight bag for me, she asked, "Would it be all right if we stopped and said hello to Mr. Button first? I've been kind of worried about him since Mrs. Button said he wasn't feeling too well."

"Sure," I said.

So that's where we went. With the cloud cover long gone, we left our hoodies at home and joined all of the people on the sunny boardwalk.

When we stepped inside the bookmobile, we found Mr. Button sitting in a chair behind the front desk. Mrs. Button was shelving books. When she saw us, she called out, "Back so soon?"

"Yep," Emma replied. "Hi, Mr. Button. You weren't here this morning, so we came to see you."

Mr. Button had lots of gray hair, slicked back, and he wore thick, black-framed glasses. He looked like someone who could teach you important things, like how the universe works and why annoying bugs like fleas exist.

He coughed before he replied, "Been under the weather the past couple of weeks, I'm afraid. Though I'm not contagious anymore. Just have this lingering cough that's making me a very unhappy man. And you know how much I love being happy."

"I do," Emma said before she burst into song, *"Don't worry. Be happy."* Then she motioned toward me. "This is my friend Juliet. She's new to Mission Beach and will start school with me next week."

"Wonderful to meet you, Juliet," Mr. Button said as he got to his feet. "Wait a second. Hold on. What in the world . . ." I started to turn around because I wondered if someone or something was behind me, but he reached out, slid his hand past and around my ear, and magically, a quarter appeared between his thumb and forefinger.

"I know we've only just met, Juliet, but I couldn't let you walk around with a quarter sticking out of your ear."

I'd seen the trick on television but had never had anyone perform it on me. He held the quarter out like he wanted me to take it, so I let him drop it into my palm.

"Thanks," I said, smiling.

He turned around and buried his face in his elbow as he coughed. When he finished, he said, "Boy, I sure do wish this awful crud would go away."

Emma chatted a bit more with him. She told him we

were having peach pie for dessert and that I was sleeping over. When we left a few minutes later, as we walked along the boardwalk toward my house, she said, "I feel so bad for Mr. Button."

I stopped walking as a big idea hit me. Two girls on Rollerblades whizzed past us.

"What? What's wrong?" Emma said, stopping a few feet in front of me and turning around.

"He wishes his cough would go away, right?" I said. "Then let's help make it happen."

Her face wrinkled up. "But . . . we aren't doctors."

We started walking again as I explained. "I know, but we can make him chicken noodle soup. And try that Vicks home remedy my mom did for me last time I was sick."

"Huh?"

"I was sick with a bad cold and missed a week of school. She put some of that stinky Vicks stuff on my feet and then made me wear socks all night. It cut way down on the coughing."

Emma wrinkled her forehead. "I'm so confused. What do your feet have to do with a cough?"

"I have no idea. All I know is it worked."

We reached my house and I got the key that was hidden in the barbecue grill on the front deck. Almost every one of the beach houses has a deck along the front, side, or back of the house. The weather is so nice most of the time, it's like another room of the house, but with no walls.

"This is so cute," Emma said when we walked in. Compared to her huge home, it probably seemed like a dollhouse. "Is your sister here?"

"No," I said. "She's always training for junior lifeguard tryouts."

Emma looked around as we walked toward my room. The walls were mostly bare in the family room. Mom had said she wanted to buy some paintings from local artists, so they'd probably be empty for a while.

When we reached my room, Emma let out a squeal at the sight of Casper, who was curled up in the middle of my bed.

"Oh my gosh, I love white cats," she said as she sat carefully next to him and petted his back. "I've wanted one forever."

"How come you don't have one?"

"My dad and Lance are allergic." She leaned down closer and looked Casper right in the eyes. "He's so pretty. What's his name?"

"Casper."

She took out her phone and snapped a photo. Then she turned and looked around the rest of my room, pointing when she noticed my *Starry Night* poster. "I'll have to get one of those. If I'm accepted into the club, I mean. By the way, do you think Some Kid will mind if I'm in on this, too?"

I went to the tiny closet and pulled out a small duffel

bag. "I don't think so. What fun is a secret club with only two people?"

"Yeah. Hopefully, you're right."

Next, Emma leaned over and picked up the family photo next to my bed. She didn't say anything.

"That was before," I said. "Obviously."

She studied it for a minute before she set it back down. "You're gonna love it here, Juliet. I know I've said that already, but I really believe it. And I want you to believe it, too."

The way she said it, it was as if she was saying if I loved it here, then I wouldn't be so sad about my parents splitting up. But I felt like I'd be sad about that for a really long time, even if living at the beach turned out to be wonderful. Sometimes, I think people forget you can be happy and sad at the same time. But the world doesn't want to see sadness, so we learn how to push it down. Hide it. Keep it a secret. Even though we probably shouldn't, because everyone feels sad now and then. Why should we be embarrassed about it?

I threw some clothes into the bag. "Once I get a few things from the bathroom, I'm ready to go."

I grabbed my toothbrush, a hairbrush, my face moisturizer, and the jar of Vicks from the medicine cabinet. Emma now stood outside the bathroom door, so I handed her the blue jar.

"So we can show Mr. Button the magic Vicks trick," I said as I stuffed my toiletries into my bag. "I think he'll be impressed. Do you know where they live, though? Like, can we show up at their house with some soup and other stuff and surprise him?"

"Yeah. My mom should know. We can ask her. And we'll have to go to the store and get the ingredients to make the soup. Do you have a recipe?"

"I'll check Mom's recipe binder before we go," I said.

Emma rubbed her hands together and smiled. "This is so exciting! We're going to try and make Mr. Button's wish come true. Clever, creative, and sneaky, that's us."

"Don't forget diligent," I said. "We have to keep trying. A bad cough probably isn't going to magically disappear overnight."

"But, but . . ." Emma whined, "I'm not that patient! I want him to get well *now*. Because he deserves it, and so do we."

"Yeah, I know," I said. "But we will be diligent. Because we have to be. Right?"

She smiled. "Yes! Diligent, that's us." She chuckled. "And maybe a tiny bit impatient, too. Nothing wrong with that, is there?"

"Nope," I replied.

As I flipped through the recipes, she said, "I've already checked my email about a hundred times since we threw the bottles in the ocean."

I side-eyed her. "Emma. Have you really?"

"No," she said, laughing. "Probably more like fifty times. I said a tiny bit impatient, remember?"

"A tiny bit," I said. "Riiiiight."

And I'm a "tiny bit"...

1. mad at my parents for splitting up our family.
2. sad that I'll never get another book recommendation from Mr. Richie.
3. in love with Vincent.
4. obsessed with lists.
5. jealous of Emma's big, happy family.
6. lucky that I got an email from someone who found my bottle!
7. quirky. Maybe. Probably.

Twelve

SOUP'S ON

On the way back to Emma's house, we stopped in at the Frozen Spoon. You can't really stop in at an ice cream shop and leave without ice cream. This time I got a scoop of chocolate chip mint and a scoop of cookie dough. Mmmm . . . so good. Along with a delicious, refreshing snack, we got the Buttons' address and Joanne's approval to make Mr. Button some soup and take it to him. She even gave us some money for buying the ingredients.

"Should we double the recipe so we can have that for dinner tonight, too?" Emma asked her mom.

"Great idea," she said. "We already have salad makings, but maybe pick up some French bread to go with it as well."

"Plus, we're having peach pie that I helped Lance make," Emma said. She turned to me. "You'll have to come over another time and have Mom's spaghetti. It's really good."

"I'd love that," I said. I knew I shouldn't be eating *every* meal with the Rentons, but I mean, who was I to turn down good food? We'd been eating out of cans a lot lately at my house.

We dropped off my bag at Emma's and then we walked to the market a few blocks away. After we got everything we needed, we went back and put all of the ingredients except the noodles in a big Crock-Pot.

When Mr. Renton came into the kitchen as we were cleaning up, it startled me a little bit. Maybe because I hadn't met him yet.

"Hi, Em," he said as he went to the fridge. "How's it going?"

"Fine. This is Juliet. Juliet, this is my dad."

He turned around and smiled. His smile reminded me of Emma's, even though the two of them didn't really look alike. I mean, he had a lot less hair than Emma, for example. As in, almost none. And he wore wire-rimmed glasses. My dad wears glasses, too. When he got new Nike frames last year, I told him maybe they'd make him go faster if he tried to run a marathon.

He'd said, "I'm pretty sure the only marathon these will help with is a reading marathon." Man, I missed my dad's jokes.

"Nice to meet you, Juliet. I'm Rick."

"Hi," I said.

Emma finished wiping down the counter and threw the rag in the sink. "She's sleeping over tonight. We're making some soup for dinner, but we're going to take some to the Buttons also. He's been sick."

Rick pulled out a small bottle of iced tea and opened it. "Very nice. I'm sure the soup will be delicious. I'll see you at dinner, okay? I'll be in my office for another couple of hours if you girls need anything."

"Okay," Emma said.

"He doesn't mind working at home with kids coming and going all day?" I asked after he left.

"Nah," she said. "He loves it, actually. Plus, no long commute and he can take a walk on the beach at lunchtime if he wants. What does your dad do?"

I liked that she asked. It would have been easy for her to ignore the subject, in case she was worried about upsetting me. But I wanted to talk about him. I mean, he was still my dad even if I didn't live with him.

"He works at the California Living Museum in Bakersfield. It's a small zoo, basically. He and my mom met at veterinary school."

"So he takes care of the animals there?"

"Yeah. The bobcats and mountain lions, mostly."

"Wow, that's, like, the coolest job ever. Does your dad let you get up close and personal with them?"

I shook my head. "No. Too dangerous. But I've taken lots of behind-the-scenes tours and been places most people don't get to go. Inca, my best friend in Bakersfield, loves it there. She'd go every weekend if she had her way."

Emma started singing. *"Make new friends, but keep the old, one is silver and the other's gold."* She smiled. "I'm so glad we're new friends, Juliet."

I laughed. "Me, too! I'm curious about something, though. Is there a reason you break out in song like that?"

She shook her head. "I'm really not sure. My mom says I've done it since I could talk. She thinks it's because, with three older siblings, it was the best way to get people to pay attention to me."

"That makes sense."

"Want to go to the beach for a while?" she asked. "We have some time before the soup's done. We could swim or throw a Frisbee or . . . sit there and do nothing. You choose!"

"Can we sunbathe and read our books?" I asked. And then I realized I hadn't planned for that. "Wait. Never mind. I didn't bring a suit."

She grabbed my hand and pulled me along behind her. "It's fine! You can borrow one of mine. This will be so fun. I haven't lain out in forever. We have to use sunscreen, though. It's one of our rules."

I followed her up the stairs. "Rules?"

"You know, safety rules, I guess. Like, don't start a bonfire without an adult around. Things like that. Some of them have changed since we've gotten older, but the sunscreen one has always been there."

"Are they, like, posted in your house or something?"

We went into her room. "Yep. Right on the fridge,

posted next to the weekly work schedule for the shop. Probably just didn't notice it."

This was a very organized family. They had a set of rules, a cool allowance program, and a weekly work schedule. Maybe when you have a lot of kids you have to be organized or life will just be constant confusion? Whatever the reason, my list-making self was impressed. And I honestly didn't mind having to obey the rules. It told me someone cared, which I liked. Yeah. I liked that a lot.

My favorite beach words

* *Mermaid*
* *Starfish*
* *Seahorse*
* *Sand castle*
* *Waves*
* *Saltwater taffy*
* *Jellyfish*
* *Coral*
* *Boogie board*

Thirteen

PART A

I carried the plastic container of soup. Emma held the bag with the loaf of French bread, a green salad, and two breath mints in a small plastic bag. She'd thrown those in at the last minute.

"Fresh breath is important, right?" she'd told me.

"You know I won't argue with that," I'd said.

I also held a small bag with the jar of Vicks along with a box of chamomile tea from the tea and coffee cupboard at Emma's house.

We'd eaten a quick meal with the Renton family and then packed up the stuff.

"It's really nice you girls are doing this for him," Emma's dad had told us as we were leaving. He was proud of her. I could tell. It had made me wish my dad knew what I was doing, so maybe he'd be proud of me, too.

When we got to their house, a white one with blue trim, Emma went to the door and knocked.

Mrs. Button answered. Before she said anything, Emma jumped in and explained why we were visiting. "We brought Mr. Button some things to help with his cough." She lifted the bags just slightly. "See?"

"Oh my goodness, that is really kind of you girls." She held the door open. "Please. Come in."

The house smelled good—like onions and peppers and spices. Emma must have noticed, too, because she said, "Have you already eaten?"

Mr. Button stepped out from the kitchen we could see partially from where we stood. He coughed into his elbow before he said, "We just finished. And it was delicious, as usual. Mrs. Button is quite the cook, let me tell you." He walked closer, throwing the dish towel he held onto his shoulder. "Now, what have you girls got there?"

"We made you some chicken noodle soup," I said. "Since you don't feel well."

He smiled. "Oh, my. Please, come in here and set it down."

As we followed him into the kitchen, I glanced at Emma. Her eyes told me she felt disappointed. I felt the same. We shouldn't have eaten first. We should have come right over as soon as the soup was done cooking.

"Oh, girls," Mrs. Button said as we put the salad, bread, and soup on the counter. "Look at what you've done. This is wonderful."

"I'm afraid I'm too full to eat again," Mr. Button said. "But it'll keep 'til tomorrow, won't it, dear?"

"Yes, yes, it'll keep," Mrs. Button said as she turned to us. "I'm really touched by your thoughtfulness, Emma and Juliet. Thank you so much."

I handed her the little bag. "In here there's some Vicks to rub on his feet at night. Cover them with socks and it'll help with the coughing."

Emma piped in. "You can also have him drink some chamomile tea before bed. Hot tea is very good for colds, you know."

"Did the two of you think of all of this by yourselves?" Mrs. Button asked.

Suddenly, I couldn't help but wonder if we'd gone too far. Maybe they didn't like people giving them medical tips. We were just kids who didn't really know anything about bad colds except what our mothers had told us.

"Yes," Emma said. "We really want to help him get better."

"We can see that," Mrs. Button said as she went to work putting the soup and salad into the fridge. "I'm certainly going to have a lot to write in my notebook of beautiful things tonight." She turned and smiled at us. "It's been a chicken soup kind of day, hasn't it? First chicken soup for feelings and now chicken soup for a cold."

We all laughed because it was strange and funny and true.

Mr. Button coughed again, and this time, it went on for a lot longer. Mrs. Button's smile turned into a frown. "I'll put the kettle on and make you some tea, Ray. You go and put your feet up."

"We better go," Emma said.

"You don't need to run off on account of me," Mr. Button said in a raspy voice.

"No, we really have to go," I said. "We're going to play Pictionary with Emma's family."

"It's spring break, remember?" Mrs. Button called from the stove.

"All right," he said as we made our way back to the front door. "You go and have fun." He coughed into his sleeve again. "Meanwhile, I'm gonna drink some tea and get my feet nice and stinky, thanks to the two of you. Good night, girls."

"Good night," Emma said.

"Good night," I echoed as we walked out the door.

The sky was a pretty golden color when we stepped out. "Wanna go watch the sun set?" Emma asked.

"Yes!" I said, happy I'd be able to cross another item off of my "Things I want to do at the beach" list.

We hurried toward the beach along with lots of other people coming out of their houses. Everyone loves a good sunset, I guess.

We took a seat in the warm sand, squinting at the horizon where the sun looked like someone had set a grapefruit on fire. It was red and glowing on the outside and a deep orange color on the inside.

"Too bad we didn't get the soup there in time," I said.

"I know," Emma said, scooping up sand and letting it slip through her fingers. "Even though soup doesn't really have magical powers or anything. It just tastes good when you're sick. Do you want to go home and write Some Kid and tell her what we did anyway?"

"I feel like I should wait," I said. "Like, maybe it would be better to tell her when we know for sure that the stuff we did helped him. That's the point, right? The email said, 'Find someone's wish. Make it come true.'"

"Basically you're saying Part A is done, Part B is not."

"Basically."

The sun inched lower, and the sky exploded with color—orange, red, and yellow. What a show. Emma got her phone out and took some photos.

"What is it about sunsets, anyway?" she asked me. "I could watch one every night for the rest of my life and never get tired of them."

I stared at the sky, watching the sun disappear. I wished I had a phone so I could take a photo and send it to my dad. Tell him the beach wasn't so bad after all. "I guess that's how it is with things you really love. You never get tired of them. Ever."

"I wish we could stay and watch the sky turn starry," Emma said as she got to her feet. "But we should probably get back."

"There's a song called 'Starry, Starry Night,'" I said as she helped me up. "It's about Vincent. Have you heard it?"

"My mom loves that song," Emma said. She started singing, *"Starry, starry night."*

I waited for more, but she turned and looked at me. "That's all I know. Maybe Mom will let me download it on my phone later."

"Hey, that should be our official club song!" I said.

"Oh, but I kind of like 'On Top of Spaghetti' for our official club song."

"So we walk around hungry all the time?" I teased. "That'd be really fun."

As soon as we walked in the front door of Emma's house, her family waved us over to the dining room table.

"Boys against girls," Thomas said. "Sit on that side."

Emma replied sarcastically, "Gee, thanks, not sure I would have been able to figure that out just by looking."

We took seats in the two empty chairs. It made me feel good that one of them was for me.

"Were Mr. and Mrs. Button happy to see you?" Joanne asked.

"I think so," Emma said, grabbing two pencils from the box and handing one to me. "They'd already eaten dinner, so they're going to have the soup tomorrow."

"He was going to put the Vicks on his feet, though," I added.

Everyone turned and stared at me. Oh my gosh. So embarrassing! I realized maybe I shouldn't have mentioned that part.

I talked fast, trying to explain it so it made sense. When I finished, Rick said, "Huh. Interesting."

"I'll have to remember that home remedy," Joanne said.

I settled back in my chair. They really were nice people.

"Okay, come on, let's play," Molly said as she set her phone on the table and scooted in. "Dad, flip the coin so we can see who goes first."

The boys won the coin toss, but I didn't care. I was just happy to be playing.

Reasons I like the Renton family

* *The Appreciation Jackpot—genius!*
* *They are loud and noisy sometimes, which is the opposite of quiet the way it is at my house most of the time these days.*
* *They love food, especially ice cream.*
* *They have rules. Sometimes rules are annoying, but sometimes they are helpful.*
* *Even when they don't get along, they still watch out for one another.*
* *They play games together.*
* *They seem to like each other (most of the time).*
* *They are nice to me, someone they hardly know.*

Fourteen

CLOSED INDEFINITELY

When I woke up the next morning, it took me a few seconds to remember where I was. The slats of the bunk bed above me clued me in. The clock next to the bed told me it was a little after seven. Early. I had no idea what time the Renton family got up, but the house seemed quiet.

After I lay there for a while, waiting to see if Emma might wake up, too, I finally got up because I had to use the bathroom. When I finished, I tiptoed downstairs to see if anyone was up yet. Joanne was in the family room, sitting in one of the chairs with a book in her lap and a cup of tea in her hands. I tried to turn around without her seeing me, but I didn't make it.

"Good morning, Juliet," she said. "How'd you sleep?"

"Fine," I said. "But I'll go back upstairs. I don't want to bother you."

She closed her book. "You're not bothering me at all. I'm the early bird of the family, along with Emma. Surprised

94

she isn't up yet, actually. Probably any time now. Do you want something to eat or drink? A glass of juice, maybe?"

I shrugged. "Okay."

She got up and I followed her into the kitchen. As she poured some orange juice, she said, "What do you like to have for breakfast at home?"

"It depends. My mom is big on protein, so eggs or peanut butter toast most days. Oh, and cereal once in a while."

Except not lately, I thought. Mom used to buy Raisin Bran or Honey Nut Cheerios for my dad. I ate the Cheerios sometimes, too, and now that she'd stopped buying them, I missed them.

"I thought I might make some waffles," she said as she handed me the glass. "If you're a waffle fan, that is."

"I am definitely a waffle fan."

"Good. Happy to have another one in the house."

"Is it hard feeding so many people?" I asked.

"I'm used to it by now," she told me as she pulled a big mixing bowl out of the cupboard. "The main thing I've learned over the years is that I expect people to tell me if there's something specific they want from the store. I keep a piece of paper on the fridge for just that purpose. We make a lot of lists around here—helps keep things organized."

"I love lists," I said. "I should tell my mom to do that. She's been so busy lately, we're lucky if she remembers to go grocery shopping at all."

"Well, meal planning and shopping take a lot of time.

95

I'm sure she's doing her best. Let me get my waffle recipe out and you can help me make the batter, okay?"

"Sure."

As she was reaching for a binder on the counter, her phone buzzed. She looked at the number. "Hm. I wonder . . . Hello?"

After a short pause, she said, "Yes, good morning, Flora. Is everything all right?"

While she listened, I watched as worry covered her face. "Oh, no. I'm sorry to hear that. Yes, of course we're glad to help. Consider it taken care of, okay?" She listened a minute before she said, "We're happy to do it, I promise. And if there's anything else, please ask." Pause. "Okay. Will you give us an update tonight or tomorrow? When you have a minute?"

"An update to what?" Emma asked quietly as she suddenly appeared beside me.

"I don't know," I whispered. "Also, hi."

She smiled. "Hi! I can't believe you got up earlier than me. You could have woken me up."

"It's fine. Your mom and I are making waffles."

Before Emma could reply, Joanne set the phone down, crossed her arms over her chest, and leaned against the counter. "That was Mrs. Button," she told us. "I have bad news."

"Oh, no," Emma said. "What's wrong?"

"She's taking Mr. Button to the hospital this morning."

"What?" Emma said while I just gasped.

"He became much more ill in the night," Joanne explained. "She didn't share any details. She called to ask if you girls might be willing to make a sign that says 'Closed indefinitely due to illness' and hang it on the door of the bookmobile. She's not sure when they'll be able to open it again."

There was that word again. *Indefinitely*. It was starting to be a very annoying word, showing up again and again when I didn't want it to.

"We can do that," Emma said as she looked at me. I noticed her hair was plastered to one side of her head. She hadn't even brushed it before coming downstairs to find me. "Can't we?"

"After waffles?" I asked.

It made her smile a little. "After waffles."

And they were *so* good. I think they cheered us up a little, even though we were still worried. Not only were they homemade but also served differently than I'd ever had them. We topped them with fresh cut-up strawberries along with a dollop of whipped cream. My new favorite!

After we finished breakfast, we got ready and made the sign. I packed my things because after we finished at the bookmobile, I'd head home. I wasn't too excited about that, but as Mom always says, it's never good to overstay your welcome.

"I feel so bad for Mr. Button," Emma said as we walked

along the boardwalk. It wasn't even nine o'clock yet, so there weren't many people out and about. From the looks of the clear, blue sky, it promised to be a really nice day.

"I hope he's okay," I said. "Will you let me know how he is? When your mom hears back?"

"Yes. You know, I also feel bad for us. We didn't make his wish come true. So we have to start over."

My heart sunk even more. "I hadn't even thought of that. Why is this turning out to be so much harder than I thought it'd be?"

"Did you answer Some Kid's email at all?" Emma asked. "Like, just to say, 'Sounds good' or whatever?"

"No. I probably should, huh?"

"Maybe write them back and tell them you're excited and you're working on it."

"Okay. I will."

"And maybe ask if it's okay if a friend helps you because she wants to be in the club, too. A really, really awesome friend."

I smiled. "All right."

We reached the bookmobile and hung the sign on the door with the tape we'd brought along. We stepped back to make sure the sign was straight and readable. "It makes me sad seeing that," Emma said.

"Me, too."

She sighed. "Hopefully, it won't be too long." Then she burst into song: *"Somewhere over the rainbow, skies are blue."*

I didn't say anything. I wasn't sure what that had to do with Mr. Button's illness.

"It's a song about hope," she told me as we turned around, back toward the boardwalk. "In case you were wondering."

"Actually, I was."

"My favorite song, too."

"I love the lion," I told her. "In the movie, I mean."

"Next time you come over, let's watch it!" she said. "We have it on DVD." She held out her hand. "Deal?"

I shook it. "Deal."

We turned toward my house. "Think you can come over again before spring break is over?" she asked.

I tried to play it cool. "Yeah. I have some stuff to do around the house. And my sister's probably really been missing me. But spring break isn't even halfway over, so I should be able to."

"Good," Emma said with a smile. "I'm glad."

Reasons I love libraries

* *They are very organized (kind of like my lists).*
* *When I find a book I like, the next time I go back, I know where to look to see if that author has any more books I might like.*
* *Certain shelves in my school library have become almost as familiar to me as my own bedroom.*
* *Doesn't matter what you look like, how old you are, if you're popular or not—anyone is welcome in the library.*
* *They make you feel welcome. Safe. Happy.*
* *Free books!!*

Fifteen

IT HURTS

I was glad to see Casper and he was glad to see me. As soon as I walked in the door, he was right there, weaving in and out of my legs.

"Okay, okay," I said, laughing. I threw my bag down and picked him up. He rubbed the top of his head on my chin. "I missed you, too."

"Hello?" I called out, wondering if my sister might be home. But there was no answer.

I walked in the kitchen and put Casper next to his food bowls. He gets canned food twice a day, at breakfast and dinner, but snacks on kibble throughout the day. He picked at the dry pellets while I read the note Mom had left me.

Hi, Juliet,
Hope you had fun at Emma's house. Please move the laundry from the washer to the dryer. And it'd

be wonderful if you could clean out the dishwasher,
too. Miranda's with friends today, training. I'll be
home in time for dinner. Might bring takeout with me.
We'll see.
    Love,
    Mom

After I did my chores, I grabbed a banana from the fruit basket and picked out a piece of light blue construction paper. I wanted to make Mr. Button a get-well card and mail it to him. I had his address on a piece of paper stuffed in my pocket. He wasn't at home, but I figured Mrs. Button could take it to him at the hospital. I drew a vase of fresh flowers with some markers and just as I was about to write the words *Get Well Soon*, the phone rang.

"Hello?"

"Juliet?"

"Hi, Dad."

"Hi. How are you?"

I wanted to say, "This is so strange, talking to you on the phone instead of seeing you every day." I wanted to say, "Mom isn't home much and neither is Miranda, but I'm doing the best I can." I wanted to say, "I miss you." But I didn't say any of that. I took the cordless phone back to the table where I'd been working.

"Fine, I guess. Did you get my email?"

"Yes, I did, honey. Thank you. And I wanted to tell you

I'm sorry you're feeling so sad about moving away. It will get better. These things just take time."

"I hope so."

"Once you start school and make friends, it won't be so bad," he said.

"I've already made one friend," I told him.

"You have? Juju Bean, that's such great news!"

"Yeah, she's really nice. And so is her family."

"Wonderful. Listen, I need to get back to work, but could you do me a quick favor? Could you give me your mom's work number?"

I paused, because it seemed like a weird question. "Can't you just call her cell?"

"I've tried. She won't answer my calls or texts. And I really need to speak to her."

I traced one of the flowers I'd drawn with my finger as I thought about what he was asking. If he didn't know Mom's work number, that meant he didn't even know *where* she worked. If he knew the place, he could have easily looked it up on the Internet.

"Dad, if you don't know where she works, maybe I'm not supposed to tell you."

"Honey, she's still my wife. And I need to speak to her."

It felt like I was being pulled in two different directions. Like Mom held my left hand and Dad held my right and the harder I tried to take my hands away, the harder they pulled. I didn't know what to do. I was pretty sure if Mom wanted him to have that number, he'd have it. But I could also see Dad's point. They *were* still married. And if he had something important to tell her, shouldn't he be able to do that?

"Are you all right, Dad? Like, is there an emergency?"

He sighed. "I'm fine. Please don't worry. But if you could just give me the number, it would help a lot. Okay?"

I went to the kitchen and opened the drawer where Mom had a list of phone numbers. Her work phone was the first one on the page. "Okay, you ready?"

"Ready."

I read the number to him, and then he thanked me and hung up. I decided I'd better call and warn her. She picked up on the first ring.

"Mom, it's Juliet."

"Oh, hi, sweetie. How's it going?" I heard papers shuffling in the background.

"Fine. But something just happened that I need to tell you about. Please don't get angry with me."

"What is it? What's wrong?"

"Dad called and wanted your work number. So I gave it to him. He'll probably be calling you soon." She didn't say anything for a long time. "Mom?"

"Yes. I'm here. Thank you for letting me know, Juliet. I need to get back to work. I'll see you tonight."

"Are you mad?"

"Not at you, no."

So that meant she was angry with him.

"How come you won't talk to him?"

"I really can't discuss this right now," she said in a rush. "Hopefully, you understand. See you later."

"Okay. Love you, Mom."

"Love you, too. Bye."

I said bye and we hung up.

And as I wrote the words *Get Well Soon* on the card for Mr. Button, I wished there was a card I could send to my parents to wish their marriage would get better soon.

Things that cheer me up

* *Videos of baby goats*
* *Watching the clouds go by and spotting an arrow or a heart or an elephant*
* *Casper just being his adorable kitty self*
* *A good book, especially one that makes me laugh AND cry because that is the very best kind of book*
* *A delicious snack like crackers and cheese or cookies and milk or anything without a boring vegetable, basically. Unless a pickle is a vegetable, then never mind.*
* *Painting a picture*
* *Glitter!!!!*
* *A walk in the sunshine with a friend*

Sixteen

MORE MYSTERIOUS

After I mailed the card for Mr. Button, I read my book about Vincent. By the time he was a teenager, he knew four languages and loved poetry. Who knew a guy born over a hundred years ago could make me feel like a slacker? Lunch consisted of another pickle sandwich with some turkey thrown in. Around three, I remembered I needed to email Some Kid.

When I logged in, I noticed Inca still hadn't emailed me back. She was probably off doing fun things for spring break. Last spring break, she'd invited me to go with her and her family to the magical land of Dole Whips, also known as Disneyland. We'd had so much fun, even if our tastes in rides were not exactly the same. Actually, we're as different as pickles and onions. I loved the rides like It's a Small World and Pirates of the Caribbean while her favorites were Splash Mountain and Big Thunder Mountain

Railroad. For her, the scarier the better. As for me? Feeling like I may vomit any second is not what I'm going for in a ride.

I opened the email from Some Kid and sat there for a few minutes, thinking about what to say. Finally, I started typing.

Hi. I'm glad you found my message. I love the idea of the Starry Beach Club. That's cool you like Van Gogh, too.

Is it okay if I have a friend who is helping me to make someone's wish come true? She's a good person, I promise. Granting a wish is a lot harder than I thought it would be. Unless you're a fairy godmother, probably.

I could pick something easy, like making my sister's wish come true of having someone take out the garbage for her when it's her turn. But I figure you want something big. Something special. So that's what we're trying to do.

Are you sure you don't want to tell us more about who you are? Like, maybe you could tell us what school you go to? That wouldn't give too much away.

Why do you want to keep it a secret anyway?

Sincerely yours,

J.J.

I read over the email approximately seventeen times, changing a little something here and there each time, until I finally decided it was good enough, and hit SEND.

Surprisingly, an email popped up from Inca, so I read that. She said she was at her aunt's house in San Francisco for a few days but was checking email on her phone. Lucky her.

"If you had a phone, we could FaceTime," she told me.

"Thanks a lot for rubbing it in," I mumbled.

They were about to go to a famous chocolate shop and have humongous ice cream sundaes. I started to tell her I had a new friend in San Diego who owned an ice cream shop so I could have ice cream whenever I wanted, when I got another notification of a new email. It was from Some Kid.

Hi, J.J.,

Yes, it's okay if your friend helps you and joins the club, too.

Why do I want to keep it a secret? I think it makes it more fun. More mysterious. Or maybe . . . I'm afraid you won't like me if you find out who I am.

Sincerely yours,

Some Kid at the Beach

Oh. My. Gosh. We might not like who she is? Or what if it wasn't a she at all? What if it really was Henry or one of his friends?

This was big news. Really big. I had to tell Emma. But I hadn't written her number down anywhere but Mom's phone. And I couldn't call Mom to get it. That'd be twice in one day and the first time hadn't gone very well. No, I'd either have to go back to Emma's house or wait until Mom got home.

I heard the door click open and turned to see Miranda bounding into the house.

"Hey," she said. "How's it going?"

I decided I wanted her to know what had happened earlier with Dad. Sometimes you need someone else in your corner, you know?

"Not very well," I said. I logged out of email and put the computer back to sleep before I turned and looked at her.

"How come?" she asked, her hair wet and stringy and her face red.

I stood up. "Dad called earlier. Wanted Mom's number at work. I didn't know what to do. I kind of figured if he didn't have it, that meant she didn't want him to have it."

"So, did you give it to him?"

"Yes. He kind of made me feel like it was his right to have it. If that makes sense? So then I called her and told her what happened, and she wasn't very happy. With him, I mean."

Miranda sighed and walked toward the kitchen. "It sucks, Pooh. This whole divorce thing? I hate it. I just want to bury my head in the sand so I don't have to hear any of it."

"Oh. So *that's* why you're spending so much time at the beach," I joked.

She went to the fridge and pulled out a bottle of Vitamin Water. "Basically, yeah." She twisted off the cap and took a drink. "They made this mess and we shouldn't be pulled into it. My new friend, Becca? She said, 'It's not your job to make it easy on them. It's their job to make it easy on you. They're the parents, after all.'"

"She sounds . . . smart," I said.

"Right?" She took another swig and set the bottle on the counter. "So when you feel pulled in two directions, remember that. Go with your gut and don't feel bad about it. Whatever happens, they're the grown-ups. They'll figure it out. Okay, I gotta jet. Time to shower and get ready."

"Get ready? For what?"

"A bunch of us are going to dinner and a movie."

So I'd be here alone. Again. Wonderful.

She started to walk away and then turned around. "You'll be okay until Mom gets home, right?"

I thought about the new email. About how I didn't have Emma's number memorized yet. About how the only way to tell her the big news was to go back to her house.

"My friend Emma invited me over for spaghetti," I told her. It wasn't really a lie. Was it? She had said I could come back for a spaghetti dinner . . . sometime.

"Okay, cool," she said. "Let's do something tomorrow. You and me. After I'm done with training."

"Sure," I said. "Now hurry up so I can shower after you."

Watching parents go through
a divorce feels like...

* *putting your hand into a box of spiders.*
* *stepping in dog doo-doo and tracking it all over the house.*
* *sleeping on a bed of sharp rocks.*
* *eating a big pile of brussels sprouts.*
* *hugging a porcupine.*
* *hopping on one foot while wearing high heels for two hours straight.*
* *going to the dentist for thirteen cavities.*

Seventeen

FAMILY DINNER

I stood on the Rentons' porch, nervously wringing my hands. I didn't want to be that pesky friend who doesn't know how to stay away. But I had to tell her what Some Kid said. I just had to. So I found the courage to knock.

A moment later, Thomas opened the door wide and said, "Hey, Juliet. Come on in. Emma's in the kitchen."

"I . . . I . . . just need to tell her something really quick."

I'd hoped he might just call her out to see me on the porch, but that's not what happened. He smiled and said, "Yeah. Whatever."

Their house smelled like something really delicious was simmering on the stove. My stomach growled, and I realized I should have waited until after dinner to do this. I kicked myself. How rude. But I was here now, so there was no going back.

I walked through the front room and then the dining room, where Lance and Molly were setting the table. They both said hi to me and I said, "Hello." When Emma heard my name, she looked up and said, "Hey! You're just in time."

"Time for what?" I asked.

"Spaghetti. You can stay, right?"

Her mom was getting a pitcher of water ready for the table. "It's no problem to set another place. Always happy to have you."

"Um . . . okay. If you're sure you don't mind?"

"Not at all," Joanne said before she called out, "Lance, can you come get another place setting? Juliet's going to join us."

So I really *was* going to have spaghetti at Emma's house tonight. And just like that, the loneliness I'd been feeling most of the day seemed to magically vanish.

I moved over and stood next to Emma at the island so I wouldn't be in the way. Emma scooped up some chopped tomatoes from the cutting board and threw them into the salad bowl. "Is everything all right?"

I leaned in and whispered, "I heard from Some Kid again. I'll tell you later."

She looked at me, her eyes big and wide. She mouthed, *Ooooh, exciting!*

Around me was a bustle of activity as people emptied pots from the stove and removed trays of hot buttery garlic bread from the oven.

"Come on," Emma said, carrying her salad. "We can take a seat."

I took my place at the table next to Emma as all of the delicious food appeared in front of us. Joanne went around and poured water into our glasses.

"Lots of help tonight," Rick said as he appeared and sat at the head of the table. "Thanks, guys. I'll take care of the dishes, how's that?"

"Good," Lance said. "I need to get ready for my date."

"Don't stay out too late," Joanne said, taking the basket of bread and passing it around. "You're opening the shop tomorrow. Emma will be there, too, helping to unpack some supplies that came in today."

"I know," he said. "I'll be home by midnight, okay?"

That sounded pretty late to me, but what did I know? My evenings were mostly spent between the pages of a book or watching TV.

As they discussed the schedules of the next few days and things that had come up at the shop recently, we passed around dishes of food. Once I had a full plate, I took a bite of the spaghetti and I thought I might pass out from the deliciousness of it. Best spaghetti of my life, no lie.

As they talked, I looked over at Emma as she wiped her mouth with her napkin. She smiled at me. "Good?"

I nodded enthusiastically. I mean, there was more food to eat. I didn't want to waste time talking.

After dinner we went up to Emma's room and sat on the soft, yellow rug in the middle of her room.

"I'm so full," I said.

"Yeah. Mom's spaghetti will do that to you." She passed me the tin of mints after taking one herself. "Okay, tell me what happened. I can hardly stand it."

I told her all about the email I'd sent to Some Kid and the response I'd received.

"The last line of the email said: 'Or maybe I'm afraid you won't like me if you find out who I am.'"

"What?" she asked, her green eyes big and round. "It really said that?"

"Yes. Doesn't that make you kind of worried? Like, what if it really is Henry or one of his friends?"

She groaned. "No. It can't be. Can it?"

"I don't know, but I wish there was a way to find out. What if this is all some ridiculous joke they're playing?"

"But why?" she asked. "Why would they do that? What do they get out of it?"

"That's what we have to figure out. Do you know where Henry lives? Maybe we should accidentally walk by."

She smiled. "Oooh, good idea. I do know. Maybe tomorrow?"

"Sounds like a plan." I glanced at the clock by her bed and when I saw the time, I jumped up. "Uh-oh. I need to get home. I wrote a note to my mom and told her I would be home by seven."

She got to her feet. "Okay. I'll walk you out."

It was almost dark outside. We probably could have

caught another sunset if we'd hurried to the beach, but I knew it was more important I get home so I didn't worry my mom.

Just as I started to trot down the steps, a young Asian woman came running over to us. "Girls, I'm sorry to bother you, but have you seen two cats wandering around here? One is gray, the other is orange and white."

"We just stepped outside," Emma said. "So we haven't really noticed anything."

The woman looked around Emma's yard, still talking. "I'm staying next door for the week while my sister and her family are out of town. And I guess I left the door open, because the cats aren't in the house anywhere. Oh, I feel terrible. I have to find them."

"Juliet has to go home," Emma said, "but I can help you look."

"Thank you so much," the woman said. "I'm Laura, by the way."

"So you're Jenny's sister?" Emma asked.

"Yes. That's right."

"I've only talked to her a few times," Emma said. "What are the cats' names, so I can call for them?"

"Pepper and Paprika," she replied.

Emma waved to me, probably figuring I needed to get going. "I'm helping out at the shop in the morning, if you want to stop by and see me. I'll be there at ten."

I waved back. "Okay. See you later."

I jogged all the way home. When I walked in the door, it was quiet. And dark. So different from the lively house I'd just left. When I flipped a light on, I found my mom sitting on the sofa, her head back. She looked tired . . . or something.

"Hi," I said. "Everything all right?"

She sighed. "Mmm. Not really."

I sat next to her. "What's wrong?"

"Just one of those days when being an adult isn't much fun."

"I'm sorry."

She reached over and patted my leg. "Not your fault, Juju Bean."

I waited a moment before I asked, "Do you think you made a mistake? Moving here?"

"No. Not at all. It was the right thing to do."

"You don't miss him? Or our home? Even just a little bit?"

She sighed. "This probably won't make sense to you, but there are things I miss about being married. Like, it's nice to have someone to help with things around the house. But . . ." Her voice trailed off.

"But what?" I asked.

"But I don't miss your father, specifically," she said. "And I'm sorry if that's hard to hear, because I'm sure you do miss him."

"Yeah. I do."

I waited for her to say, "I'm sorry," but she didn't say a word. A minute passed, the two of us just sitting there in the silence. It was so sad. So quiet. It made me miss my old life more than ever. When she finally spoke, she asked, "Are you hungry?"

I swallowed the lump in my throat. "No. I ate at Emma's. She asked me to stay when I ran over to tell her something."

"That was nice."

"Yeah. We had spaghetti. It was really good."

"I'm glad."

"I wish I could have brought some home. Did you get takeout? Want me to dish some up for you?"

She leaned her head back again and closed her eyes. "Mmm. That's sweet, thanks. I should probably eat. It's on the counter. And I got extra fortune cookies, so help yourself."

"Okay. Be right back."

As I pulled the cartons out of the white paper bag, the fortune cookies tumbled onto the counter. I picked one up, ripped open the plastic, and cracked the cookie open. It read: *A very big wish is about to come true.*

I should have been happy about that one. I mean, that's what Emma and I wanted, wasn't it? To make a wish come true. But all I could think about was the wish I'd had ever since we'd heard the news in February: that my parents would get back together. That we could be a family again. A month ago, I would have held on to hope that this meant maybe it might come true. But the more time that went by, the more I knew the chances of that happening were really, really small.

Smaller than a ladybug's wing.

Smaller than a watermelon seed.

Smaller than the tip of a fine-point pen.

I stuffed the fortune into my pocket. Hopefully, someone else's wish could come true even if mine never would.

Some of my other wishes

* *World peace*
* *Life on Mars*
* *For animals to live forever*
* *A library in every neighborhood*
* *Flying cars*
* *That love never ends*
* *To be a part of something special*

Eighteen

BIG DREAM

The next morning, I was eating peanut butter toast when someone knocked on the front door.

"Surprise!" Emma said when I answered. She wore jeans and a pink T-shirt that said POWERED BY ICE CREAM. "So glad you're awake." She pointed to my wet head of hair. "You don't even have to use a blow-dryer? Lucky."

"Nah, I just didn't feel like it," I said. "Anyway, come in. What's going on?"

She stepped inside and I shut the door. "Two things. First, Mrs. Button called this morning."

"And?"

"And poor Mr. Button has pneumonia."

"Oh, no! That's terrible."

"Yeah. He's going to be in the hospital for a few more days, at least."

"I made him a card and sent it to their house," I said.

"That's so nice. My mom said she's going to send some flowers to the hospital from all of us."

"I bet he'll like that."

"And the second thing is I wondered if you have some time right now to help me before I go to work."

"With what?" I asked.

"I want to look for those cats some more. Laura is really worried about them. And she's afraid to tell her sister because she knows how upset she'll be. She just wants to find them before she comes back."

"Yeah. I can help. Just give me a minute."

While I was in the bathroom brushing my teeth, Emma called out, "You didn't tell me you like to paint. Juliet, these paintings are *so* good!"

I finished up and went out to the family room and over to the shelf where a couple of my paintings were on display. One was an owl and the other was a tree. I'd signed them with my name at the bottom, so it wasn't hard for Emma to figure out who'd painted them.

"Thanks," I said. "I'm definitely better at painting than gymnastics."

"Will you paint me something someday?" she asked. "For my room? I'd love it so much. And I can pay you if you want."

I smiled. "Oooh, my first commissioned piece."

"What's that mean?"

"When you pay an artist to make you something. But you don't have to pay me. I'm just joking. You're a friend. I can do one for free."

"Awesome."

I grabbed my hoodie and said, "Okay, I'm ready."

We went through the neighborhood to get to her house this time, rather than the boardwalk, so we could look for the cats. A couple of times Emma called out, "Here kitty, kitty, kitty." Nothing happened the first time. The second time, a scrawny tabby cat came running out to us. He was so friendly. He let both of us pet him for a minute before he turned and went back to wherever he'd come from.

When we turned onto Emma's street, we saw Laura out front along with a man and a woman. As we came closer, Laura waved at us, a big smile on her face. "Girls, I have good news. The cats have been found, thanks to Mr. and Mrs. Moon. They found them hiding under their back deck. All the knocking on doors paid off."

"I'm so happy you got them back," Emma said.

"Me, too," I said.

"They must have slipped under there last night," Mr. Moon said. "Our dogs went straight there this morning when we let them outside. I put them back in and was able to lure the cats out with some canned tuna."

I smiled. Tuna fish always saves the day!

"Well, we better get going," Mrs. Moon said. "We have an appointment."

"Oh, but please wait," Laura said. "I want to give you something. A thank-you gift." She turned to us. "You, too. I'll be right back."

In about thirty seconds, she came back carrying three small jelly jars filled with something that did not look like jelly at all. She handed one jar to the Moons and the other two to Emma and me. "Spicy Korean sauce. I made a new batch yesterday. It's good on grilled meat or vegetables and rice. Or anything, really. Well, not fresh fruit. That would be terrible. But, hopefully, you like spicy?"

"Love spicy," Mr. Moon said. "Thank you! See you later."

"Bye," Laura said. She turned to us. "I hope you girls like spicy, too. Or someone in your family, anyway."

"Can't wait to try it," Emma said.

"Me, too," I echoed. Again. Emma was always one step ahead of me in the figuring-out-what-to-say department. Maybe when you live in a big family, you learn how to speak up or you get left out.

"I love to cook," Laura said. "I've always dreamt of opening a small Korean restaurant. I so admire your family's ice cream shop, Emma. That takes a lot of work."

Emma glanced at me with her eyebrows raised. Then she turned back to Laura. "Do you want to talk to my mom or dad about it? Like, ask them questions or whatever?"

"Oh, no. I don't want to bother them."

Emma pulled out her phone. Probably checking the

time. "I actually have to go to work right now," she said. "You could come with me if you want. My mom will be there. I know she wouldn't mind."

Were we going to try and make Laura's dream of opening a restaurant come true? That seemed like a really *big* wish—one that would be hard to make happen. Especially when she was only visiting for a week.

Laura turned and glanced at the house. "Well, I guess I could. The cats are safe and sound inside now, and I don't have anything else going on. Let me just lock up and I'll go with you."

"Okay," Emma said.

As soon as she left, I said, "Are you thinking what I think you're thinking?"

"That this could be the most amazing wish to make come true ever?" she said.

"But . . . a whole restaurant?"

She scowled. "Juliet, what's wrong with a restaurant?"

"Nothing," I said, realizing I might have hurt her feelings. "I didn't mean it like that. What I meant is that it would take a long time. Right?"

She bit her lip. "Oh."

"I don't want to have to wait a year to find out who Some Kid is."

"Okay, well, we can still help her. Can't we?"

Laura strolled down the drive. "Okay. I'm ready." She looked at me. "Are you coming with us, too?"

Emma didn't even wait for me to reply. "Yes. She's going to help me unpack some supplies. It'll go so much faster that way. Then we have something important we have to do." She looked at me and wiggled her eyebrows. I knew she was talking about going to Henry's.

Hopefully, we'd be better at figuring out if Henry was Some Kid than we were at finding missing cats.

Things I'm not very good at

* *Finding lost things*
* *Slicing cheese evenly off the big brick*
* *Gymnastics*
* *Tennis*
* *Softball*
* *Maybe anything athletic*
* *Thinking of the right thing to say quickly*
* *Waiting patiently for the next book in a series I love*
* *Remembering to leave a note when I'm rushing out the door*

Nineteen

A FAVOR

"His house is over there," Emma whispered, like we were spies on a secret mission. Which we kind of were, I guess, even if it didn't seem very secret to be walking around in broad daylight. "The light green one."

Just as I was about to say, "Looks like no one's around," Henry came running out the door and down the steps. When he reached the sidewalk, he spotted us.

"Hey," he called, his hand on his forehead to block the sun.

Emma waved. "Hey, Henry."

"What are you doing here?"

"We're, um, taking a walk," she said.

"Isn't it more fun to walk on the beach?" he asked, looking both ways before crossing the street and coming over to us. "Can't write notes to any mermaids here."

"She's showing me around the neighborhood," I said

quickly. "Sometimes the boardwalk gets really crowded with all the tourists."

"Yeah," he said. "It does."

"What are you up to?" Emma asked, crossing her arms.

"I have to do my sister a favor." He rolled his eyes.

I glanced at Emma, because this sounded suspicious to me. "What kind of favor?" I asked.

"She wants me to get her a book at the bookmobile," he said. "She wrote the title down and said she'd pay me five bucks to go and get it for her."

"Is it about Vincent van Gogh?" I asked before I could stop myself.

He looked at me like I'd just asked him if he was going to have sea urchins for lunch. "No. Not even close. Why would you say that?"

"Juliet's obsessed with his artwork, that's all," Emma said. "You've heard of him, right?"

"I think so," he said. "He cut off his ear, didn't he? Because he was so depressed?"

Emma wrinkled her nose. "Ew, who cares about that? His paintings are some of the best in the world."

"Whatever," he said. "I gotta go. See you later."

"But wait," I called out as he started walking away. "The bookmobile's closed. Mr. Button's in the hospital."

He turned around. "Really?"

"Yes. Really," Emma said. "You'll have to go to the regular library."

His shoulders slumped. "Aw, man. Okay. I'll get out my bike. Thanks for letting me know."

"Any special reason why you're doing her a favor?" Emma asked. I wanted to say, "Like, because she's writing some emails for you?" But I didn't.

He grinned. "Maybe because I'm a nice person?"

"Nope," Emma said. "Must be another reason."

I couldn't help adding, "Did she do a favor for you first, and so you're paying her back?"

He shook his head. "You girls are so nosy. Why does it matter?"

Emma turned to me. "I think we're barking up the wrong tree, as my dad likes to say."

"I love that saying," I said. "And you're probably right."

"You know what I think?" Henry asked as he turned back toward his house. "I think you've been talking to the mermaids a little too much."

It made me smile. We probably did sound a little bit crazy.

"Bye, Henry," Emma called out. "See you Monday in P.E. I know you can't wait."

He just shook his head and kept walking.

"I don't know if he's the one," I said. "But he's definitely acting suspicious."

"Right?"

"Hey, what time is it?" I asked.

"I'm starving, so definitely lunchtime," she said as she

pulled her phone out. "It's almost one. You want to come back to the house with me for a sandwich?"

"No, I should get home," I said. "I forgot to leave a note when I left. My sister might be wondering where I am."

"Okay," she said. "Sorry we're not any closer to figuring out who Some Kid might be. Or to making someone's wish come true. At least Laura was happy to have her questions answered, right?"

"Yeah. I'm glad about that," I said. "She's really nice."

You know who wasn't very nice, though? My sister. As soon as I walked in the door, she yelled, "Juliet, where have you been?" She was on the couch, remote in hand. "I've been here, waiting for you, for like an hour. I thought we were going to do something?"

"Sorry, I was at Emma's."

She shut off the TV and got to her feet. "Why didn't you leave a note?"

"She came over this morning and asked me to do her a favor. I didn't know I'd be gone so long. I'm really sorry."

"You live here, not there, you know," she said in a sharp tone.

Before I could reply, there was a knock on the door. Since I was closest to the door, I answered it. There stood Mr. Dooney, in his striped cap, holding a bouquet of pretty white flowers wrapped in a plastic bag with water at the bottom.

"Good afternoon, young ladies," he said. "I'm

Mr. Dooney, as you may know. I hope I'm not intruding. I just wanted to say welcome to the neighborhood." He reached out and handed me the flowers. "I know your grandparents quite well. Your grandma dropped me a postcard to let me know your family would be moving in here. If there's anything you need, please don't hesitate to ask, all right?"

"Thanks," Miranda said, coming over to where I stood. "That's really nice of you."

"What kind of flowers are these?" I asked, planting my nose right in the center of the bouquet. Their fragrance was rich and sweet. "I love them."

"Gardenias," he said with a sad smile. "I grow them in my yard. They were my wife's favorite."

I didn't know what to say. Obviously, his wife wasn't around anymore and that made him sad. Fortunately, my sister stepped in. "It's nice of you to bring us some. Thank you."

He sort of peeked around us. "Looks like you're pretty well settled. Will you tell your mother I stopped by to say hello? And I really do mean what I said. If you need anything, all you have to do is ask."

"We'll tell her," I said. "Thanks again."

We said good-bye and I closed the door. I turned to my sister. "I need to eat. I'm so hungry, I'm about ready to start munching on these flowers like a horse."

"Okay," she said with a sigh. "Go eat. But, Juliet, next time you run off like that, either call me or leave a note, okay?"

"I know, I know!" I put my nose in the flowers again as I walked to the kitchen. "Hey, can you come help me find a vase, please? I don't know where she put them."

I opened two cupboard doors with no success while Miranda marched in and went to the correct spot the first time. She handed me a gorgeous blue one.

"Just say it," she said. "I'm amazing."

I gave her a smirk. "Are you going to tell Mom?" I asked as I filled the vase with water. "That I left without telling you where I went?"

"I don't know yet," Miranda said.

"I said I was sorry," I reminded her.

She came over to where I stood and went to work arranging the gardenias. "I know."

"Do you think Mr. Dooney heard us arguing?" I asked as I pulled out a box of mac and cheese.

"Maybe," she said. "I opened the windows when I came home."

"How embarrassing. He probably thinks we're two horrible children with a single mom who's never home."

She grabbed a pot and filled it with water for me. "Or he thinks we're two normal sisters who fight sometimes."

"Mom and Dad fought sometimes, and look what happened to them," I said.

She turned to me. "They were fighting a lot more than sometimes. You know that. And in between the fights, there'd be days or even weeks when they wouldn't talk to each other *at all*. And Dad had been sleeping on the couch in his study for who knows how long. It wasn't normal."

As hard as it was to admit it, I knew she was right. I'd tried to push all of that away. To pretend it hadn't been that bad or that it didn't matter very much. But they had both seemed pretty miserable not long after my birthday last year.

It was quiet for a minute before I asked, "But . . . we're normal? You and me?"

"Not gonna lie, sometimes you get on my nerves big-time, Pooh," she said as she put the pan on the stove. "But guess what."

"What?"

"You're the only sister I have. And even if I don't always like you, I always love you. So basically, you're stuck with me."

I couldn't help but smile. "Good."

"Now hurry up and get your lunch made so we can get out of here and do something," she said, marching out of the kitchen. "I'll be waiting out on the deck."

I almost said, "You're not the boss of me," like I've said hundreds of times since I could talk. But this time, I didn't. I just said, "Okay. Be there in a few."

Reasons I love my sister

* She makes really good chocolate chip cookies.
* She knows every Taylor Swift song by heart.
* Sometimes she'll help me with my homework if I bribe her with a painting.
* She has three of my owl paintings hanging in her room.
* She calls me Pooh and I call her Pooh and no one else is allowed to do that.
* I can browse her bookcase anytime. Well, as long as I ask first.
* She's not afraid of hard things, like becoming a junior lifeguard.
* She knows how to make me feel better. Usually.
* She hates pickles, which leaves more for me.

Twenty

TACO NIGHT

Miranda and I spent the afternoon at the amusement park at the end of the boardwalk. It was a lot of fun. She used some of her allowance on tickets so we could go on rides and play games. The one downside? I got sunburned because I forgot to put on sunscreen. If only I had a list of beach rules memorized, like Emma.

When Mom got home later that night, we talked about our day over a dinner of tacos and rice. Yes, she actually brought home ingredients to make a meal. Amazing.

"Mom," Miranda said shortly after we'd started eating, "I really think Juliet needs a phone."

All of a sudden, I wanted to take back every mean thing I'd ever said about my sister.

Mom sighed. "Girls. We've talked about this."

Miranda continued, "I know, but she forgot to leave a note this morning when she left the house. I came home and didn't know where she was. It was pretty awful."

Wait, never mind, every mean thing I'd said about her is completely true!

"Where'd you go?" Mom asked me.

"To help Emma with something," I said. "She came over and we had to hurry because she needed to get to work soon. I'm sorry I didn't leave a note. I forgot, that's all."

"Juliet, I'm getting worried you're making a nuisance of yourself with that family," Mom said. She picked up her glass of water. "I feel like you've been spending every spare moment over there."

Great. More of this from Mom, too? I felt anger rising up inside of me like a big wave about to hit land. "Mom, what am I supposed to do? Sit around here by myself? Sometimes, being alone is fine. But I shouldn't have to do it all the time. I feel like you moved us here and then . . ."

"And then what?" she asked.

"Basically deserted us," I said quietly, staring at my half-eaten taco.

Mom put her water glass down hard. "That is not fair. You know I have to work. I have to work so I can pay for your art supplies and the cable TV you love to watch and this dinner we're eating. What do you expect me to do?"

I tried to stay calm as I answered, but my voice shook a little and I had to blink back tears. "How about letting us stay in the town where we know people? *Lots* of people. And where we have a mom *and* a dad?"

She put her face in her hands for a moment before she got up with her plate in hand. She looked so angry, with her lips pursed and her cheeks red. "You need to understand that I'm doing the best I can. And someday, when I'm able, I'll try to explain to you why I felt we had to move here. But in the meantime? I would appreciate it if you give me a little slack, please." She moved toward the kitchen and then turned around. "I'd like both of you to stay home tomorrow, please. Do some laundry. Clean the kitchen. Read books. Take naps. Just . . . chill. I'll be home late because I'm going out after work. I'll leave you money to order a pizza. Got it?"

"Okay, Mom," Miranda said, staring at me like I'd just caused the sky to fall.

All I could do was nod.

"I'll be in my room," Mom said. "Good night."

After she left, Miranda leaned in and hissed at me, "Why'd you say that?"

"What?"

"That she moved us here and deserted us? It wasn't very nice."

I didn't want to argue anymore. I didn't want to feel like I was wrong and everyone else was right, because that feeling? It's horrible.

"Sorry," I mumbled as I got up from the table.

I rinsed off my plate and put it in the dishwasher, along with Mom's, since she'd left it in the sink. There was still some taco meat on the stove, so I scooped it up and put it in a plastic container.

I thought back to taco dinners with Dad. Whenever he made them, he always heated up a can of corn, too, because he liked corn on top of the lettuce with the tomatoes. I used to make fun of him whenever he did it. I felt my stomach tighten up at the thought. I shouldn't have done it—made fun of him like that. I bet Emma never made fun of her dad and the way he did certain things. She probably loved everything about him, the way I should have loved everything about my dad when I had the chance.

Now it was too late. He was there and I was here and whenever he had tacos with corn on them, he probably cheered because I wasn't around to make fun of him.

Miranda came into the kitchen, her eyes kinder now. She probably wanted to have some sisterly heart-to-heart talk, tell me how I needed to give Mom a break, but I wasn't in the mood.

"See you tomorrow," I said as I walked past her toward my room.

"Pooh?" she asked.

I stopped but I didn't turn around. "What?"

"I had fun this afternoon." She paused. "And I'm sorry I've been gone so much this week."

Trying to figure out what to say with all of my mixed-up feelings felt like trying to clean up a gallon of spilled milk with a single napkin. Hard. So I didn't say anything except "Good night."

I went to my room, shut the door, and picked up the Vincent van Gogh book. I wanted to read about someone else's sad life for a while. That would make me feel better. It almost always did.

Facts about Vincent van Gogh

* *He was 27 years old when he did his first painting.*
* *He used peasants as models.*
* *When he ran out of money to pay the models, he started painting more landscapes and flowers, and even himself.*
* *Some of his best work, including* The Starry Night, *he painted while staying in a mental hospital. He painted* The Starry Night *as he looked out the small window of his room just before the sun came up.*
* *He mostly traded his artwork with other artists for food or drawing supplies. It wasn't until after his death that he became famous.*
* *It sounds like he loved his brother Theo more than anyone else in the world. They're buried next to each other in a cemetery in a small town in France.*
* *Theo was with him when he died and said Vincent's last words were "*La tristesse durera toujours." *In English it means "The sadness will last forever."*

Twenty-One

SEA TURTLE

It felt like Mom had grounded us, and I didn't understand why. Was it really because she didn't want me bugging the Renton family? I wished she understood that they didn't mind. And if it made me happy to be there instead of home where I wasn't very happy, why not let me be happy?

I was angry and confused. When I finally left my room the next morning, I found Miranda in the kitchen, making blueberry muffins. Not with fresh blueberries. Muffins from a box.

"I ran to the market and thought I'd make these," she told me. "Just add an egg and some milk and that's it. So easy, right?"

She was way too chipper for nine o'clock in the morning. "Do I really have to stay here today?" I asked, crossing my arms over my chest as I leaned against the counter.

"Yes," she said. "I'm not going to lie to Mom for you."

"Well, can we at least go to the beach?"

She pointed to my very pink arms. "I think you got enough sun yesterday. Should probably stay inside today."

"But I don't want to," I moaned.

"Let's clean up the kitchen after I put these in the oven," she said. "Then we can paint. I'll paint with you, how's that?"

Normally, painting made me happy. But the way I felt, I just didn't see it happening.

"Mom is being so unfair," I said. "She's, like, punishing us for no reason. And what's with her going out after work tonight?"

Miranda set the whisk down and turned to look at me. "You know what, Juliet? If you want to be miserable, go to your room and be miserable by yourself. I don't want to be around you when you're like this. It's not fun."

"Well, I'm sorry I can't be happy all the time like Emma, who has a big happy family she gets to live with while I'm stuck here with you!" I screamed. And then I stormed out.

I lay on my bed next to Casper and cried. I thought of Vincent and his last words—*The sadness will last forever.* Sometimes, it really did feel that way.

A while later, Miranda knocked on my door.

"Come in," I said. The tears had stopped. Now, I mostly felt numb.

"Here," she said as she set a plate with two muffins next

to my bed, along with a glass of milk. "You'll feel better after you eat something."

She picked up the birthday photo from my nightstand and stared at it for a minute before she set it down. "I miss him, too, you know. And I get it. It's hard, leaving everything we loved, but we have to try and make the best of it."

I scooted up and leaned back against the headboard. Then I picked up a muffin and bit into it. It was warm and soft and tasty. "I know," I said after I swallowed.

"I cleaned up the kitchen," she said. "Let's get dressed and go to the beach."

"Really?"

"Yeah. We'll slather on sunscreen before we leave."

"Will you help me build something in the sand?" I asked, thinking about my list of things I wanted to do at the beach.

"Like what?"

"A sea turtle?"

She shrugged. "I guess we can try. It may just look like a big lump in the sand, though."

"No," I said. "We can do it. I know we can. It'll be the best thing ever."

It was not the best thing ever. More like the hardest thing ever. Even though I'd printed out some pictures of sea turtles made out of sand and brought them with us, we couldn't get the mound of sand to look like the back of a turtle.

I groaned as I lay back onto the cool, wet sand, exhausted and frustrated. I closed my eyes, the sun too bright for me to do anything else.

"Do you want to call Emma?" Miranda asked. "See if she wants to come and help us?"

"Pretty sure that would be against Mom's rules for the day," I said.

"I hope you can see I'm trying to make you happy," she said.

I sat up with a sigh. "I know." I stared at the sea turtle in the making. "I think we need a big piece of cardboard or something. To smooth it out better."

"We could go home and cut up a moving box," Miranda said. "Or we could go get an ice cream cone and see if they have something we might be able to use while we're there."

"Ice cream?" I asked. "We haven't even had lunch yet."

She gave me a half grin. "Maybe today should be backward day. You remember those, right?"

How could I forget? They were amazing. Mom would have a meeting or something and leave Dad in charge.

Even though I remembered it all really well, it was comforting when Miranda kept talking. "Dad and cooking are not friends," she said with a smile. "So when he was in charge of dinner, he'd put it off and put it off—"

"Until we were starving," I said.

"So he'd give us dessert first," Miranda said, "to buy himself more time to make something."

The first time he set bowls of ice cream in front of us before we'd eaten a healthy meal, Miranda and I were shocked. And ecstatic. I could still see his face so clearly when he exclaimed, "It's backward day! How about that, girls? A special new holiday."

"Backward day," I mumbled, staring out at the beautiful blue ocean.

"It'd make Dad proud," Miranda said.

I got to my feet and brushed sand off my legs below my shorts. "Yes, it would. Let's go."

Emma and her mom were in the shop along with Thomas. It was a little after eleven, so they'd just opened. We were the only ones there.

"Hey," Emma said, her hair pulled back into a short ponytail. She leaned the broom she'd been holding against the wall. "Looks like you guys have been having a lot more fun than me this morning. Digging a hole to China, maybe?"

"That probably would have been easier," I said. "We're trying to make a sea turtle in the sand. We wondered if you might have some cardboard we could use? We need something big to smooth the shell out better."

Thomas started moving toward the back room. "I'm on it. Let me get you some different-size pieces. Some curved, some square. Be right back."

"We also came to get ice cream," Miranda said.

"Worked up an appetite, huh?" Joanne said, her eyes

practically twinkling. "Let me know what you'd like when you're ready."

Both of us strolled along the cases, checking out the flavors.

"Mom," Emma said. "Can Juliet sleep over tomorrow night? We wanted to watch *The Wizard of Oz*." She tried to talk like a Munchkin. "Follow the yellow brick road. Follow the yellow brick road!"

I laughed.

"Fine with me," Joanne said.

Emma turned back to me, talking fast. "I'd have you stay tonight but I have plans with my friend Lenora this afternoon. Hopefully, tomorrow night's okay?"

I glanced at Miranda, wondering if she'd make up some excuse as to why I wouldn't be able to. But she didn't say anything.

"Can I let you know tomorrow?" I asked. "I'll have to ask my mom."

"Yes," she said. "Call me. Text me. Email me. Whatever."

"I don't think I have your email," I said. "Do I?"

A look crossed over her face. A funny look. A *really* funny look.

"Oh, that's right," she said as she reached back and nervously tugged on her tiny ponytail. "You don't. I'll have to give it to you sometime. Remind me, okay?"

"Yeah. Okay."

Miranda pointed to something in the case. "Can I get a scoop of that red velvet, please?"

"You bet," Joanne said. "Have you decided what you'd like, Juliet?"

"I'll just have vanilla, please," I said.

Anything else was too complicated at the moment. Because all I could hear inside my brain was, "What if Emma wrote you the email? WHAT IF EMMA WAS ACTUALLY SOME KID?"

Could Emma be Some Kid?

* *It is a little fishy that I got a reply from Some Kid so soon.*

* *Except Emma was with me—how could she have gotten my message?*

* *Maybe she read over my shoulder when I wasn't looking. Maybe she pretended to write a message, but the whole time she was actually watching me write mine!*

* *OR maybe she asked her sister to get the bottle for her. She did text someone right after we left the beach.*

* *Why would she do it, though? Maybe just to make something exciting happen instead of a whole lot of nothing?*

* *If it's true, she's a really good actress. When I showed her the email that she might have written, she looked shocked.*

* *But one thing that's never made any sense to me— why did she have two bottles that day? What if she was specifically looking for someone like me? Someone who was so desperate for friends, she'd believe any old silly email that came her way?*

Twenty-Two

HEART CHANGE

With the help of some simple pieces of cardboard, the turtle actually turned out all right. Better than terrible, at least. I mean, let's be real, it'd never win a contest—but at least it looked like a turtle. Sort of. The legs were too small and the head was too big, but when we finally finished, we stood back and admired our handiwork.

"I'm glad we didn't give up," Miranda said as we stood there.

"Me, too," I said.

And that was that. We went home and collapsed. Ate pizza for dinner. Went to bed early because there was nothing else to do. I read for a while, but it was hard to focus because I kept thinking about the funny look on Emma's face when I told her I didn't have her email address.

It reminded me of the time my sister got caught lying about being at a basketball game when she was actually at a friend's party. Miranda had left the twenty-dollar bill Mom had given her on the kitchen table. So, wanting to make sure Miranda didn't go hungry (because watching teen boys play basketball apparently makes you ravenous?), Mom went to the game to give it to her. But Miranda wasn't there. And Mom was furious.

The next morning, over breakfast, Mom asked her, "How was the game?"

Miranda said, "Fine."

"Who won?" Dad asked.

"Oh, uh, I don't know," she said, fidgeting with her napkin and blinking really fast. "I left a few minutes before it was over."

I'd heard my parents talking the night before, so I knew Miranda was lying. But even if I hadn't known, I think her face would have given it away. She looked . . . nervous. And that's exactly how Emma looked when I'd corrected her on the email address. Like she was hiding something.

But why would Emma do it? That's what I didn't understand.

When I woke up Saturday morning, I immediately got up and made scrambled eggs and toast. Along with the plate of food, I put a cup of coffee and one gardenia in a little vase on a serving tray and took it into Mom's room.

I softly nudged the door open with my hip. Sunlight streamed through the blinds. Mom was awake, sitting up in bed, looking at her phone. As soon as she saw me, she smiled. "Juliet, oh my gosh, what have you done?"

After I put the tray down, I sat on her bed. "I know it was a hard week. New house. New job. Moody daughter."

She reached out and touched my cheek. "You know, it occurs to me you have every right to be moody. A lot has happened."

I felt a little better, hearing her say that. Sometimes you just need to know someone sees you.

She took a sip of coffee. "Did you and your sister have a nice day yesterday?"

"We did," I said. I didn't want to keep anything from her, or lie, so I told her all about the sea turtle. "Even though it was frustrating, getting it right, we had a pretty fun day together."

Mom smiled. "I'm so glad. That's exactly what I wanted." She took a piece of toast and bit into it. "Want the other piece? I doubt I can eat both."

I shrugged. "Sure."

She handed it to me and kept talking. "You and your sister need to be there for each other right now. More than ever. This full-time job of mine is going to be a bit hard on all of us, but the good news is that you two have each other. And that is no small thing."

I nibbled on the toast. "I know."

She smiled before she took a bite of eggs. "Good. So I

thought we'd go shopping today for some new school supplies. Make sure you two start off on the right foot on Monday. As in, let's throw away that binder that's basically being held together by packing tape and get you something better."

"Can I ask you something?"

"Of course, sweetie."

"Promise you won't get mad?"

"Mmmmm . . . okay."

"Emma invited me to sleep over tonight. And I really, really want to. She said we could watch *The Wizard of Oz* together and some other fun things. I know you're worried I'm bugging them, but they really don't care. Like, seriously. They don't."

While I talked, she finished her eggs. Then she washed them down with more coffee and wiped her mouth with the napkin I'd put on the tray. Finally, she said, "I think what I'd like to do is meet Emma's family for myself. Or at least Emma's mother. That would probably make me feel better. What do you say?"

"Sure! When do you want to go? We could stop by the ice cream shop. Joanne is always there when it's open, I think."

"How does she do that?" Mom asked. "Work there all the time, I mean?"

"I think that's why they aren't open in the evenings. Well, except sometimes in the summer. I've only heard them talk about it a little bit, but I'm guessing it's a lot easier when it's only six hours a day instead of ten or whatever."

"That makes sense," she said. She moved the tray to the end of the bed. "Okay, let's get ourselves ready and head over there when they open. You want to shower first or shall I?"

"You can. I can just rinse off in the ocean." Before she could tell me I would *not* be doing that, I said, "I'm joking. I'll go after you."

When we arrived at the Frozen Spoon at eleven, Joanne greeted us with a big smile. "Good morning, Juliet. I'm afraid Emma isn't here today."

"That's okay," I replied. "My mom wanted to see your shop and to meet you."

"Wonderful," Joanne said as she came from behind the counter out to where we stood. "It's so nice to meet you. I'm Joanne." She turned and motioned as she said, "And that's my daughter Molly."

"Hello," Molly said, her long brown hair pulled up into a messy bun on top of her head.

"Nice to meet you as well," my mom said to Joanne. "I'm Wendy. I wanted to thank you for being so kind to Juliet."

"Well, the pleasure is ours, I promise," Joanne said. "We've loved having her around." She looked at me. "Are you staying over tonight? Emma is already planning an elaborate Emerald City meal."

"That sounds interesting," Mom said. "Do you know what's on the menu?"

Joanne chuckled. "All I know is that when I left, she was busy making bicycle wheel pasta salad." She made a circle with her thumb and forefinger. "The pasta is shaped like a bicycle wheel. Because Miss Gulch rides a bike, you know. So clever, that Emma."

Oh my gosh. Who even does that? Plans a creative meal to go along with a movie? Obviously, Emma, that's who. I looked at my mom. "Is it all right?"

"Sure. Sounds like fun. I still want to take you and Miranda shopping this afternoon, though." She turned back to Joanne. "Is there anything she can bring tonight, to help with dinner?"

"Oh, no. Actually, I probably shouldn't have ruined the surprise. I hope Emma isn't upset with me."

"I'll act surprised," I told her. "It should be pretty easy since I don't know what else she's planning to go with the pasta salad."

"Sounds good," Joanne said. A family of four stepped into the shop. Joanne greeted them and then turned back to us. "So nice to meet you. I'm glad you stopped in to say hello."

Mom said, "Thanks again for your hospitality. We'll get out of your way now. Take care."

We said good-bye and went back outside.

"She's very nice," Mom said.

"Can I borrow your phone?" I asked her. "I need to call Emma and tell her I can come. What time?"

Mom fished her phone out of her big, black purse. "Hm, how about three? That should give us enough time to shop."

"We're gonna shop for notebooks for that long?" I asked as I put in the ridiculous pass code to get to the contacts.

"Well, I'd love to walk on the beach for a bit, if you don't mind. I haven't been able to enjoy it since this first week here has been so busy. Then we need to do some grocery shopping, too. And . . ."

Her voice trailed off.

"And what?"

"I've had a change of heart."

I was about to hit TALK but waited. "What do you mean?"

"I think here, in this new place, where it seems I need to allow you to have more independence, a phone might be a good idea after all."

I admit, I squealed. Pretty loudly. Then I said, "Really, Mom? Really?"

"Yes. Really."

"Thank you, thank you, thank you!"

I threw my arms around her, almost dropping the phone, which would have been terrible. Nothing says "I'll be really responsible with my own phone" like dropping your mother's.

After I hugged her, I called Emma. "I can sleep over," I said. "As long as you don't mind if I bring my brand-new phone with me!"

Times in my life when I've been surprised

* *When I made a hole-in-one playing miniature golf*
* *When I tried taco pizza and it wasn't gross*
* *When my dad played the ring toss game at the county fair and won the stuffed giraffe I wanted more than anything else in the world*
* *When Inca and I got a $20 bill from a lady who stopped at our lemonade stand and told us to keep the change*
* *When I rode the Snow White ride at Disneyland and was kind of terrified*
* *When I learned mixing two primary colors makes a completely different color*
* *When Dad told me owls have three eyelids for each eye*
* *When I found out people who love you can still disappoint you, even if they don't mean to*

Twenty-Three

SUPER SNEAKY

Along with bicycle wheel pasta salad, we had broomstick corn dogs, a big plate of colorful fruit in the shape of a rainbow, Emerald City green salad, and for dessert, star-shaped Rice Krispies Treat magic wands. I took a photo of the spread and texted Mom and Miranda so they could see it for themselves. Of course, my very first text on my brand-new phone involved food.

It was so much fun to eat the foods inspired by the movie and talk about our favorite scenes while we ate dinner. I couldn't believe Emma had gone to all that trouble for me.

As we ate, I felt guilty even thinking Emma might be tricking me about who answered my message. Still, I knew this sleepover was my chance to find out for sure, once and for all. How did I plan on doing that? I had absolutely no idea. Maybe I'd wave one of those magical Rice Krispies Treat wands and I'd suddenly know whether she was or wasn't Some Kid. If only.

"Maybe this should be a monthly tradition," Molly said as she helped clear the table. "A movie-themed meal and a viewing party."

"No. Please," Thomas said. "We have enough traditions."

Enough traditions? It made me curious. "Like what?" I asked. We had traditions around Christmastime, but that was about it.

"Oh, let's see, there's the green pancakes for breakfast on Saint Patrick's Day. We have to have pies on National Pi Day. And cupcakes on National Cupcake Day. Once a month, we gather in the same spot on the beach and take a photo. Oh, and there's Family Reading Night every Monday."

"Those aren't really traditions," Emma said. "Are they? They're just . . . fun things we do as a family."

I thought about that for a minute. *Fun things we do as a family.* What fun things did I do with my family? We used to go on hikes together. We used to have a picnic in the backyard on the last evening of the school year, complete with sparkling cider, to celebrate. We used to have a big Fourth of July celebration on our cul-de-sac.

I hated how everything was "used to." Did Mom miss those things? Did Dad? The first week after they told us they were splitting up, I spent a lot of time in my room, remembering the fun times we had together and crying because there wouldn't be any more of them. Not with all four of us. No more vacations. No more family dinners. No more holidays.

But here, the Rentons had so many traditions, or fun family things, or whatever you called it, someone was actually worried they had *too* many.

"The definition of tradition," Lance said, reading from his phone, "is the transmission of customs or beliefs from generation to generation. So, yeah, those might not really be traditions."

Emma turned to me. "Lance is our family word nerd."

"Hey," he said, sweeping his hair back with one hand while he stuffed his phone into his pocket with the other. "Words matter. And when you don't know what one means, why just guess when you can look it up and know for sure?"

Maybe a definition was another one of those "detailed things," like book titles, Emma didn't care much about. Or maybe she liked guessing?

"Well," Emma said as she gently grabbed my arm, "we could stand here all night and discuss traditions and movie-themed dinners, but Juliet and I have important business."

I stared at her, trying to figure out what she meant. "We do?"

"Yes. We have a movie to watch with a cowardly lion, a wicked witch, and flying monkeys. Remember?"

"Ohhh, right," I said. "I almost forgot." Because I was too busy thinking about how much I missed having a complete family. But I didn't tell her that.

I followed her upstairs to the bonus room. Emma shut

the door, dimmed the lights a little with a fancy dimmer switch, and turned the television on. "I haven't had time to look for the DVD. It'll take me a minute to find it. Someone should step up and alphabetize our collection."

I decided this was my chance.

"While you look, I'm going to use the bathroom, okay?"

She opened two of the doors on the entertainment center and peered inside. "Yeah. Sure."

When I left the bonus room, I could still hear voices downstairs, which was a relief. I needed all of them to stay down there a little while longer so I could properly snoop in Emma's room without getting caught.

Once in her room, I immediately looked for the beach bag she'd had that day we'd met. Maybe she had a note inside where she'd jotted down her plans or something. After searching around the room and under her bed, I opened her closet. The bag hung on a hook on the door. Inside the bag I found an old, smelly beach towel, three different bottles of sunscreen (because Emma takes the beach rules very seriously), one of the library books we checked out from the bookmobile, a couple of extra pieces of blue ribbon, and a small notebook with a pencil attached.

I grabbed the notebook and flipped through it. There were lots of pages of doodles. Only a few pages had actual writing on them—two pages were lists (yay, lists!) and the other was a page of math problems, like she'd used the notebook for scratch paper while doing homework. There wasn't anything about the bottles or a secret club or anything. I put the notebook away, hung the bag on the hook, and shut the closet door.

As I walked back to the bonus room, I knew there was only one way to find out for sure if Emma was Some Kid. I needed to sneak downstairs to the family computer in the middle of the night, while everyone slept, and see if I could find any emails sent to my email address.

My stomach twisted into a knot at the thought. But what other choice did I have?

My favorite things from The Wizard of Oz

by Emma

1. *Aunty Em*
2. *A dog named Toto and a picnic basket*
3. *Munchkins*
4. *A scarecrow, a tin man, and a lion*
5. *A rainbow*
6. *Ruby-red shoes*
7. *Glinda the good witch*
8. *A star-shaped wand*
9. *A big, high crown*
10. *The shiny yellow brick road*

Twenty-Four

TRUE CONFESSIONS

What if the computer has a password on it?

What if someone gets up for a warm glass of milk (yuck)?

What if there's a burglar alarm I don't know about and it goes off?

These are just some of the questions that swarmed my brain like a bunch of angry bees as I lay there waiting for it to get late enough so I could head downstairs. I knew Emma was already asleep because she was snoring. Not super loud or anything. In fact, it was kind of a funny snore—a soft little gurgle every now and then.

She snored. I worried. I tried to distract myself by making my own list of favorite things from *The Wizard of Oz*, but I couldn't really focus.

Emma had asked me if I wanted to charge my phone overnight, but I told her I still had a lot of battery life left. Really, I'd wanted to keep it with me because it had a flashlight and I'd need it to get through the house.

I checked the time. It was now a little after one. I knew her siblings might stay up into the wee hours of the morning, but I figured they'd be in their rooms and wouldn't see me. And if they did, I could say I needed a drink of water.

The longer I lay there, the more anxious I got. The thing was, I knew it was wrong to snoop, especially on something like a computer. And the more I thought about it, the more I knew the idea of Emma being Some Kid was kind of ridiculous. Maybe she really had thought she'd given me her email address. It was an easy mistake. Wasn't it?

And maybe there was more than one way to find out. One that was much better than spying on someone's private emails. I threw the covers off the bed, and while I held my phone, I climbed up the ladder to the top bunk. I crawled over and sat against the railing.

"Emma?" I whispered, touching her arm. "Emma, can you wake up? I need to ask you something."

She moaned and rolled over. "What? What's wrong?"

"Your sister didn't run and get my bottle out of the ocean, did she? And then give it to you?"

Emma sat up. I turned on the flashlight and held my phone facedown so it wasn't too bright but we could see each other a little better. Emma did not look happy.

"You think my sister is Some Kid?" she asked.

"Um, not really."

She was quiet for a moment. I could almost see the gears in her brain spinning. "You think *I'm* Some Kid?"

"It's just, you looked surprised when I told you I didn't have your email address. Like you'd let something slip. And the person writing the emails does sound like you. Kind of."

"I can't believe . . ."

Her voice trailed off. Her very disappointed-sounding voice.

"Juliet, why would I do that?" she asked. "It doesn't make any sense."

"For the fun of it? Because you were worried someone would never write to me, and you wanted to pretend that someone did?"

She shook her head. "For the fun of it? For the fun of lying to you? I can't believe you'd think I'd ever do that."

I hung my head. The way she spoke to me, I couldn't believe I'd think that either. What was wrong with me? I wanted to cry. To run away. To go back home and never think about any of this ever again. I felt awful. But I knew if I did that, if I ran away, I'd lose a good friend. A friend who had been extra nice to me from the very first moment she'd met me. So I decided to tell her.

"Okay, the thing is? I have this thing about lies," I said, my voice shaking. "I hate them. I hate them so much. My parents told us they'd never get a divorce. And now that's what they're doing. And so I guess I'm more suspicious than I should be. Because it hurt so much. Does that make sense?"

"Yes," she said, putting her elbow on her leg and resting her chin in her hand. "It does. My mom and dad always tell us that trust has to be earned."

"What does that mean?" I asked.

"It's like, before your mom let you get a phone, you had to show her that you could take good care of hers sometimes. It's the same with people. You want to believe everything I say, but we haven't known each other that long. So I have to show you that I mean what I say. And that I don't make things up for the fun of it."

"Well, thanks for not being mad. I'm really sorry."

"Thanks for telling me what happened," she said. "Everyone has a thing, you know?"

"A thing?"

"Yeah. Like, I have this thing where I get tired of being with my family all the time, but I hate being alone. That's why I love being with friends. I told my mom once that it seems like I should love to be by myself. But unless I'm reading, I don't really like being alone. And now I know you have this thing where you don't always believe what people tell you. Everyone has a thing. Sometimes a few things. It's just the way it is."

"Yeah," I said with a yawn. "I guess you're right."

She yawned, too. "Think you can go to sleep now?"

"Yes," I said. "I'm suddenly *so* tired."

"Okay. Get to sleep. We have a lot to do tomorrow."

"We do?"

"Yes. It's the last day of spring break."

"I know. So what are we doing?"

"We have to find a wish to make come true. Then we can email Some Kid and finally have an ending to this mystery."

A real friend is...

* *Forgiving*
* *Understanding*
* *Loving*
* *Easy to talk to*
* *A good listener*
* *A treasure*

Twenty-Five

BIKE RIDE

The sound of a door closing woke me up. I rolled over to see if someone was in the room, but I didn't see anyone.

"Emma?" I asked.

No answer. I figured she went to the bathroom, so I lay there thinking about our middle-of-the-night conversation. When I'd crawled back into the bottom bunk, it had felt like we were okay. Like she wasn't upset with me. But sometimes things change. What if she'd thought it over and had decided she shouldn't forgive me so easily after all?

Once, Inca and I got in an awful fight. Another girl at school, Chelsea, told me something Inca had said, something terrible. Chelsea said Inca had told her I was weird and the only reason she was my friend was because she liked going to see the animals at the California Living Museum, where my dad worked. It hurt my feelings so much. We were at school when she told me, and I went to the bathroom and cried. I ignored Inca for a couple of days, until she finally came to my house almost in tears, begging me to tell her what she'd done wrong. When I told her what Chelsea had said, she got really mad.

"I can't believe you thought I'd said that," she'd said. "Why didn't you ask me if I did instead of believing it so easily?"

I didn't know how to answer her. I told her I was sorry, but it took a long time for us to get back to normal.

Why was it so easy for me to believe the worst in people? It didn't make sense. Emma seemed to be the perfect friend. Me, not so much. And if Emma had lots of friends, it would be so easy for her to let me loose. I was like a kite that looked fine in the store but didn't fly so well once you tried it out.

I got out of bed and got dressed. Emma walked in a minute later.

"Hey," she said.

"Hi."

She raised her eyebrows and said, "I have an idea. Have you ridden bikes on the boardwalk yet?"

"No," I said. "But I really want to."

"Sunday mornings are a good time to do it. Not as busy. You can ride Molly's bike if you want to. But first let's have a doughnut. Dad just got back from the bakery."

"Okay." I swallowed hard before I said, "Emma, I want you to know, I really am sorry. About what I told you last night."

"I know," she said. "Except you probably can't sleep over ever again."

I stared at her, shocked.

Then she laughed. "Juliet, I'm joking! It's fine. Really."

I scowled. "That wasn't funny."

Her smile disappeared as she said, "Sorry. My bad."

"At least I know you're not perfect now."

She looked at me funny. "Perfect? What do you mean?"

"You're one of the nicest people I've ever met. You have the perfect life, with the perfect family."

"No," she said. "I'm not perfect at all. Like, my siblings are always telling me I ask way too many questions. And they're probably right. But I can't help it. I'm curious."

I didn't want to argue about perfection. It didn't matter. My mom was always telling me there's no such thing as perfect. I reached over and gave Emma a hug. Then I said, "Owning an ice cream shop is pretty perfect, though."

She smiled. "It's sweet. Not perfect. But definitely sweet."

After breakfast, I texted Mom and asked if it was okay if I stayed and rode bikes on the boardwalk with Emma. She said it was fine but she'd like me home for lunch at noon.

"That gives us two hours," Emma said. "Lots of time."

As we got out the bikes, Emma told me the boardwalk was three and a half miles total. We rode away from the carnival stuff, toward the other end, since I hadn't seen much that direction. It was sunny, though not very warm, since it was still early in the day. I was glad I'd worn jeans and a hoodie.

"Are you excited about school tomorrow?"

"Excited? More like terrified."

She laughed. "I'll show you around. Don't worry. And you can sit with me and my friends at lunch."

I felt the terror decrease a little. Lunchtime was the thing I'd been dreading the most.

"I hope we have some classes together," I said.

"Me, too," she said.

She told me about some of her classes as we rode, in case I wanted to try and request any of them. Sometimes one of us would have to move ahead and ride single file if the boardwalk got too crowded. But it was fun chatting and riding and looking at all the different houses on one side, and having the beach and ocean always on the other.

It took us an hour and a half to get down and back. I was just about to tell her I was starving when Mr. Dooney waved at us and yelled, "Good morning, girls."

Emma hopped off of her bike, so I did the same. Classical music drifted through the windows of his bungalow and something about it made me feel . . . sad.

"Hi, Mr. Dooney," Emma said. "How are you?"

"I was feeling quite melancholy this morning. It seemed strange, since it's a beautiful day and I have wonderful leftovers to eat for lunch. Then I remembered. My sixtieth wedding anniversary is coming up on Wednesday."

Emma reached for her phone and tapped on the keyboard. She explained, "I'm looking up 'melancholy.' Lance's habit has finally rubbed off on me, I guess."

"Aw, I see," Mr. Dooney said. "Those phones are something else, aren't they?" Mr. Dooney turned to me. "My wife passed away, you see. I miss her. Every year, there are hard days, but the date of our anniversary is especially difficult. I feel like I'd like to celebrate somehow, but that's silly, isn't it? She's gone. I have to let it go."

Emma read the definition. "The definition of 'melancholy' is: a feeling of pensive sadness, typically with no obvious cause." She looked up from her phone. "So when you woke up, you felt sad but didn't understand why. Until you remembered the anniversary."

"Yes," he said, taking his hat off and scratching his head. "That's it."

"I'm sorry," Emma said.

"Me, too," I said. I told myself to make him a card later. He'd probably like it if people remembered the special day.

"This is her favorite song," he said, as the music continued to play. "'Clair de Lune.' She played it so beautifully on our piano. It's been five years since I've heard it played in my house. I sure do miss it."

As soon as he said it, I knew. I knew as sure as the sun rises every morning and sets every night. We'd found our wish.

Steps my brain goes through when I have an idea

1. *That's a fantastic idea!*
2. *Well, it's a good idea.*
3. *No, maybe it's a bad idea.*
4. *What if it's a bad idea?*
5. *It's probably a really terrible idea.*
6. *Maybe I need to tell someone to find out.*
7. *I have to tell someone to find out!*

Twenty-Six

NOTHING EXTREME

When we got back to Emma's house, I decided to just say it and get it over with. "I think I know whose wish we should grant."

She squinted her eyes in that curious sort of way. "Whose?"

"Mr. Dooney's," I said. "We should find someone to play 'Clair de Lune' on his wedding anniversary."

"Ooooh. That's such a good idea." She wrinkled her nose. "Or . . . wait. Maybe it's too sad? Like, will it make him miss her even more?"

"Yeah, that's what I was wondering," I said. "But you heard him, right? He misses hearing that song on his piano."

"But don't you think he meant he misses hearing it played by his wife?" she asked.

I felt my phone vibrate in my pocket. I pulled it out to find a text from Mom. *Time to come home, please.*

I texted her back to let her know I was on my way.

"Let's sleep on it," Emma said as we went up the steps to her house. "My dad says when you're unsure about something, it's good to let it sit a while. He says time and space can often give you clearness. No, that's not it. Clarity? Another word for clearness, right? Anyway, let's talk about it tomorrow at school."

I missed my dad giving me advice like that. When someone gives you advice, it shows they care. It shows they want what's best for you, even if the advice isn't always the kind you want to follow. Sometimes, it might even sound ridiculous. Like when my dad told eight-year-old me I should learn how to change a tire. I think he meant *someday* I should learn to change a tire, but at the time, I thought he meant I should learn right then. Which didn't make any sense because I'd never seen a single eight-year-old in my entire life off the side of a road changing a tire.

I told Emma, "Okay. We'll sleep on it. I just hope we have enough time to find someone to do it."

I ran upstairs, grabbed my overnight bag, and came back down.

"See you tomorrow, I guess," I told Emma.

"The sun will come out tomorrow," she sang.

"Okay, Annie," I said. "If you say so. Sun or rain, I'm really glad you'll be there."

"Yep. Me, too," she said as she held the door open for me. "Bye."

"Bye."

On the way home, a soft breeze blew and the smell of the sea air made me smile. I went over outfits in my mind for my first day at a new school. Should I wear a skirt and dress up a little bit? Or should I just do jeans and a cute T-shirt, and try not to stand out? Or maybe I'd wear my new yellow pants we'd bought shortly before we left Bakersfield. Yellow pants seemed like a very San Diego thing to wear.

"Hello, Juliet," I heard someone say. I spun around to find Mrs. Button walking up from the beach, wearing a floppy straw hat and carrying sandals in one hand and a book in the other.

"Hi!" I said. "How are you? How's Mr. Button?"

She walked up to where I stood and then, together, we moved to a sidewalk off the boardwalk so we wouldn't be in people's way. "I'm fine. And he's doing much better, thank goodness. The antibiotics are doing their job."

"Is he still at the hospital?"

"No. He's at home. He's resting now, so I thought I'd come and get a little fresh air. Been cooped up inside so much lately." She smiled. "Juliet, the card you made him brought a smile to his face. Thank you for that."

"You're welcome," I said. "I wish I could do more."

"The outpouring of love and support we've received has been wonderful," she said. "I've certainly had no lack of material for my notebook of beautiful things."

"Do you think you'll open the bookmobile soon?" I asked.

"Probably in another week or so. I hope. Too difficult for me to leave him now."

I wondered if my question made me seem impatient. I didn't mean it that way. "It's okay," I said. "People understand. I was just curious."

"Yes, I know. Well, I'm off to say hi to Mr. Dooney. This will be a hard week for him. His sixtieth wedding anniversary is coming up."

"I know," I said. "He told us." I paused, wondering if I should ask her. I decided it couldn't hurt. "Emma and I were talking about doing something for him on Wednesday. Since it might be a sad day for him. You think he'd like that?"

"Depends on what it is," she said. She put her sandals on the ground and slipped one foot in, and then the other. "I don't think anniversaries can really be celebrated when one of the partners is gone. But that doesn't mean you can't do something for him to let him know you're thinking of him." She stood up and smiled at me again. "It's a very sweet idea. Just don't do anything too extreme, right?"

"Right."

We said good-bye and as I walked the rest of the way, I thought about what that meant. I even used my phone to look up the word *extreme*, but it didn't really help. It gave synonyms like *maximum*, *extraordinary*, and *exceptional*. Why would something extraordinary be bad? I didn't understand.

I felt more confused than ever about whether we should

try to find someone to play the song for Mr. Dooney on his piano. He hadn't wished for it, exactly. But he had said he missed it. Wasn't that the same thing? Like, every day, I woke up and missed seeing my dad. Did I wish I could see him? Yes. I did.

When I walked in the door, my sister, standing in the kitchen with Mom, said, "About time. Did you get lost or something?"

"No," I said as I took my bag to my room. "I saw Mrs. Button, so we stopped to talk."

"Who's Mrs. Button?" Miranda asked.

"She and her husband run the bookmobile," Mom said. "Remember?"

I went to the table and sat down at my spot. There was a sandwich and some chips waiting for me. I checked to make sure there were enough pickles. There weren't. But I took a bite anyway.

"Is Mr. Button feeling better?" Mom asked.

I nodded while I finished chewing. "He's back at home. But the bookmobile won't open for another week, at least."

"Well, now you'll have the school library to get books," Mom said.

"I know," I said. "But I love the bookmobile so much. It's really cute. You two should go there when it reopens."

"Maybe I will," Mom said. "Even though I don't have much time to read these days. Oh, that reminds me, I'm going out Tuesday night. I'll make sure and have something easy for you girls to make for dinner."

"Where are you going?" I asked.

"Dinner and a movie," she said. "With some friends. I'll go after work, so I won't see you until later."

"Okay," Miranda said. "We should call Dad tonight, Juliet. Didn't he say he'd like to talk to us every Sunday?"

I felt the familiar pain in my chest. Talking on the phone wasn't as fun as seeing him around the house. I missed talking about silly things like grasshoppers and stinky socks and what kinds of apples taste the best—in person. On the phone it was just the boring small-talk stuff. It wasn't the same. It'd never be the same.

Things that remind me of my dad

* *Stinky socks (because he has stinky feet)*
* *Cookies and milk (because he loves them)*
* *The color forest green (because it's his favorite)*
* *Tennis balls (because he loves to play)*
* *Calvin and Hobbes (because he owns at least ten books)*
* *The smell of rain (he always goes outside after a rainstorm)*
* *Corn and tacos and Honey Nut Cheerios, but not all together. Gross.*

Twenty-Seven

CRABBY CRAB

After lunch, I got on the computer and found a YouTube video that had the song "Clair de Lune." It is such a pretty song. I listened to it three times and then I made a list about how it made me feel.

When that was done, I checked email and found two new ones, one from Inca and one from Some Kid. I could tell from the date that Inca had written it before I'd bought my cell phone. Now she had my number so we could text. I opened the one from Some Kid.

Hi, J.J.,

I haven't heard from you. Is everything okay? Do you still want to be a part of the Starry Beach Club? If not, I'll find someone else. The more I think about it, the more I realize the world really needs us. People wish and they wish and they

wish. But sometimes, it's just not enough. They
need help. I want to help. Don't you?

Sincerely yours,

Some Kid at the Beach

I wrote her back right away.

Dear Some Kid,

Yes, I still want to be a part of the club. It's just
that my friend and I are trying to find a really good
wish. It's not as easy as you might think. Maybe
along with being clever, creative, sneaky, and
diligent, we need to be patient, too. Just an idea. I
might have some good news for you Thursday.
Cross your fingers!

Sincerely yours,

J.J.

After I shut off the computer, I was about to go paint a
picture to give to Emma, since she'd wanted one so badly.
But Miranda said we should call Dad. Mom had gone down
to the beach for a while, so it was a good time. We sat on
the sofa together and she called him on FaceTime. After
we talked about the weather and boring stuff like that, he
told us they'd received a new tortoise and a new porcupine
at the zoo.

"Do they have names?" I asked.

"We're working on it," he said. "I think they might do a contest for the kids to name them."

"Can I see them?" I asked. "When we visit? And maybe take Inca with us?"

"Yeah, yeah, of course," he said.

This wasn't how it was supposed to be, though. I'd always gone to welcome the new animals a day or two after they'd arrived. It'd almost become like a family tradition, now that I thought about it. Yes, it'd been exciting for me as a kid, because I loved animals, but I'd wanted to do it for other reasons, too. I knew the animals must be missing home and I'd wanted to say hi, and tell them it'd be all right. Maybe they couldn't understand my words, but I wanted to believe they could understand the message.

Funny thing was, now *I* was the one missing home.

We talked a little longer and then he said he had to run some errands and needed to get going.

"Love you, girls," he said. "Have a good first day tomorrow."

"Love you, too," we said in unison.

And then we hung up.

I sighed, leaned my head back against the couch, and closed my eyes.

"What's wrong?" Miranda asked.

"How come talking to him always makes me feel worse?" I asked.

"Hmm," she said, getting to her feet. "Maybe because you haven't really accepted this is how it's going to be? You really need to accept it, Pooh. Stop fighting it. Stop wishing it were different. It doesn't do any good."

I opened my eyes and stared at her. "Did you ever think it might be easier for you because you have something here you've dreamt about forever?"

"What do you mean?"

"Junior lifeguarding," I said. "But what do I have?"

"Well . . . you have a new friend, right?"

"I know, but—"

Before I could finish, Mom walked through the front door with messy hair and pink cheeks. She looked relaxed. Happy, even.

"I love it here," she said with a sigh as she threw her beach hat on the coffee table. "Don't you love it here? There's just something about the ocean that is so therapeutic. I can literally feel my soul healing."

Meanwhile, my soul felt like a volcano that was about to erupt. And erupt it did.

"Is that why we moved here?" I shouted as I stood up. "Because your soul needed healing? Well, what about mine, Mom? What about my soul? Did you ever think about that?"

Before she could answer, I fled to my room faster than a sand crab trying to bury itself after a breaking wave. Mom was probably even calling me crabby right then. A crabby crab, for sure.

I lay on my bed and buried my nose in a book, in case she came in to talk to me. Talking was the last thing I wanted to do. Though I didn't really feel like reading, either. I was too upset to read. Too upset to do anything. But I read the same paragraph over and over, trying to calm myself down while also trying to make sense of what the words said.

Finally, after enough time had gone by and it seemed like Mom had decided to leave me alone for now, I texted Inca.

> My dad said the zoo got new animals. A tortoise and a
> porcupine.

She responded right away. I want to go see them! Thanks for letting me know. Want to FaceTime right now?

I told her maybe later. I didn't give a reason, but the reason was I didn't want to miss home any more than I already did.

As I lay there thinking about it, it made me wonder about Mr. Dooney and his anniversary. If Emma and I found someone to play his piano, would it make him feel better or worse? I wanted to believe it would make him feel better, but what if it didn't?

The last thing I wanted to do was turn Mr. Dooney into a crabby crab. One in the neighborhood was enough.

Listening to "Clair de Lune" feels like

* *Floating on a cloud*
* *Hugging a rainbow*
* *Watching a pink-and-orange sunset*
* *Eating a strawberry fresh from the field*
* *The opposite of crabbiness (which is why I listened to it on my phone over and over again)*

Twenty-Eight

BEACH WISHES

Mom pretended the argument never happened. We all pitched in at dinner. Set the table. Ate dinner together with the television on. Did the dishes. And then went our separate ways. Our house felt sad and lonely.

I thought about running away to Emma's house and asking if I could just move in with them. I'd do my share to help with things. I wouldn't bother anyone. Maybe I could even learn how to make a piecrust better than Emma. I could bake a pie every night and that way no one would mind having one extra kid around.

As I set out my clothes for the next day, there was a knock on my door. I felt my muscles tense up.

"Who is it?" I asked.

"Me," Mom said as she opened the door and poked her head in. "Can I come in?"

I shrugged. "Whatever."

She came and sat on the edge of the bed. "Cute outfit,"

she said as I set the short-sleeved navy shirt with little daisies all over it next to my yellow pants.

"Thanks."

"Honey?"

"Yeah."

"I know this hasn't been easy," she said. "And I want you to know I did think of you and Miranda when I decided to move us here. I thought about all of us. And I felt that this was the best thing for us."

"But why?" I asked, sitting on the opposite side of the bed.

"Because it can be hard getting asked about your personal family business everywhere you go. Between your father and me, we know a lot of people in Bakersfield. I didn't like the thought of us being whispered about wherever we went. Or, for the people who hadn't heard the news, being asked, 'How's Bruce doing?' and having to explain over and over that we'd separated."

I hadn't thought of it that way—that people would be curious. "Is that the only reason?"

"No, of course not," she said. "I thought the beach would be good for us. Not just me, but you and your sister as well. With everything else feeling so uncertain, it seemed to me that it might be comforting to walk outside and see the beautiful ocean there, day in and day out. A constant source of serenity, perhaps."

"Serenity?" I asked.

"Peacefulness. And really, if you must know, Grandma is the one who said as much, and convinced me to move."

"She did?"

"Yes. She did. But please don't be upset with her. She only wants good things for all of us. Sometimes a change of scenery is necessary, honey. That doesn't mean it's easy. But in the long run, I'm hoping we all benefit from being here." She scooted over and wrapped her arms around me. "Juliet, do you want me to see if you can visit your dad next weekend, even though it's not a scheduled visit? Would that help with the missing?"

It was such a surprise, and I couldn't believe how happy it made me.

"Yes," I said right away. "Yes, it would."

And just like that, I knew we should surprise Mr. Dooney with that special song. Because sometimes a really good surprise is exactly what you need.

Mom took me to school the next morning and got me enrolled. Emma and I ended up having P.E. together and that was it. Since we were busy playing basketball, we didn't have much time to talk. At lunchtime, we sat with some of her friends, so we couldn't really talk then, either. But after school, we both took the bus home, and she sat next to me so I could finally tell her.

"I think we should do it," I told her.

"Do what?"

"Find someone to play that song for Mr. Dooney."

"Really?" she said. "I was thinking we shouldn't."

"No," I said firmly. "We definitely should. I really think it'll help him with the anniversary. Does your family know anyone who plays the piano?"

"Um . . ." She stared out the window for a moment. "Yes! My sister has a friend who plays really, really well. I know because Molly went to her recital once. Her name is Kari. I'll get her number and ask her when I get home."

"Thanks," I said.

"If she says yes, what do I do? Have her meet us at Mr. Dooney's house after school on Wednesday?"

"Yeah. That sounds good. Maybe I'll make cupcakes and bring those, too."

"I think we should invite Mr. and Mrs. Button to be there," Emma said. "They've been friends with Mr. Dooney a long time."

"Good idea."

She suggested we go to their house later that afternoon, so instead of going home, I went to Emma's, and thanks to my new phone, I texted Mom and Miranda to let them know. We had carrot sticks with hummus for a snack while we told Molly about our idea for a surprise on Mr. Dooney's anniversary. She gave us Kari's number, so Emma called her and explained our idea. Emma offered her a pie, any kind she wanted, for doing us this favor, and Kari said she'd happily do it for an apple one.

"Isn't there anything else you need done?" I asked Emma. "I'd love a berry pie for payment."

"You know what, when berries come into season, I'll make you one for no reason." She started beatboxing. "And look at me, making a rhyme, I'm that good, all the time."

I laughed. "Yes. You are."

With the piano player taken care of, we decided to walk to Mr. and Mrs. Button's house and invite them to join us on Wednesday. A woman next door was washing her car in the driveway.

Emma called out, "Hi, Jenny."

Jenny waved. "Thank you so much for introducing my sister Laura to your parents. She said it was really great getting some of her questions answered about owning a restaurant."

"You're welcome," Emma said. "Hope she does it someday."

"I think she will," Jenny said. "Thanks again."

As we walked, with the warm sun on our skin and the feeling that we were close to finally making someone's wish come true, my heart felt like a kite soaring inside my chest. What we'd be doing for Mr. Dooney felt exactly like the kind of wish Some Kid had wanted us to find. It wasn't super obvious. It wasn't even something Mr. Dooney had specifically asked for. We'd just put the pieces together and realized there was something we could do to make him happy.

I remembered Some Kid's words: "Maybe the stars need helpers now and then."

Wednesday night, the stars would be smiling down on us, the helpers. I was sure of it.

Favorite Kinds of cupcakes

* *Strawberry Lemonade*
* *Chocolate Peanut Butter*
* *Banana Cream Pie*
* *Red Velvet*
* *White Chocolate Raspberry*
* *Okay, any kind as long as there's no raisins or coconut. Ew.*

Twenty-Nine

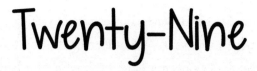

PRETTY MAGICAL

"Hello, girls," Mrs. Button said, her notebook of beautiful things in one hand and her reading glasses in the other. "So nice of you to stop by, but I'm afraid Mr. Button is sleeping now."

"That's okay," I said. "We just have something really quick to tell you."

"Well, in that case, I can step outside with you for a minute."

After she shut the door behind her, Emma said, "We're going to surprise Mr. Dooney with a little something on his anniversary, and we thought maybe you and your husband would like to come."

She smiled. "A surprise? Are you going to tell me what it is?"

Emma and I looked at each other. "I think we want to wait and have you see it for yourself," I explained. "But it's nothing too extreme. It's nice. You'll see."

"Well, it's very kind of you girls to plan something. It will certainly be a sad day for him. Anything we can do to lift his spirits will be appreciated, I'm sure. Count us in. Or me, anyway. It's hard to say how Mr. Button will be feeling."

"Okay," Emma said. "We understand." She pointed to the notebook. "It's been a hard week with him being sick, hasn't it? How do you find things to write about?"

"Oh, there are always beautiful things to write about," she said. "All I have to do is look out the window, really." She slipped her reading glasses back on, then opened the notebook. "Here are a few of the things I've written today. Sunshine like a sweet lemon cake and clouds like fluffy buttermilk frosting. Birds scampering across the yard, joy sprinkled on the tips of their wings. Daisies in bloom: the ordinary flower which provides extraordinary happiness."

"You make me want to live inside your notebook of beautiful things," I said.

Mrs. Button winked. "It's all in how we see things, isn't it?" And then she turned back toward the door. "See you girls on Wednesday. After school, I presume?"

"Yes," Emma said. "We'll run home, drop off our stuff—"

"And pick up the cupcakes," I said, cutting in. "Then we'll be right over."

At the word *cupcakes*, Mrs. Button grinned and gave us a wink. "What a treat this will be. I can't wait to see what you have planned." She waved. "See you Wednesday."

"Bye," we said.

As we walked down the cute little street, Emma said, "We see the boring old sun while she sees a sweet lemon cake." A dog barked in the distance. "How does she do that?"

"I don't know," I said. "But it's almost like magic, isn't it?"

"If you think about it," Emma said, "we're going to be in a secret club that makes wishes come true. That seems pretty magical to me."

I'm not sure why, exactly, but I couldn't stop thinking about what Mrs. Button had read to us. Every time I saw a bird, I tried to see joy sprinkled on the tips of its wings . . . but they looked like ordinary wings to me. Where did she come up with the joy part? What made her think of that? I really wanted to know.

Tuesday after school, I went to the store and bought a cake mix and frosting to make red velvet cupcakes. Miranda went to the beach after school for lifeguard training, and by the time she came back, the house smelled like a bakery. Delicious.

"Are these to take to Mr. Dooney's tomorrow?" she asked when she walked into the kitchen.

"Yes," I said. "We can each have one tonight, though. I want to make sure they taste okay. Should we wait until after dinner?"

Dinner would be pasta with some Trader Joe's marinara sauce. All we had to do was cook the pasta and heat up the sauce.

"I'm thinking it's another backward night," Miranda said as she reached for a cupcake. She handed it to me and then picked out one for herself.

I wasn't going to argue with that. I hadn't frosted the cupcakes yet, so I popped the lid off the tub of vanilla frosting, grabbed a butter knife, and smeared frosting on the one I was holding. I handed the knife to Miranda, then peeled off the paper and took a bite.

"Mmmm," I said. "Really good."

She stuffed half the cupcake in her mouth and gave me a thumbs-up.

"So ladylike, Miranda," I said.

I got out the milk and poured us some. When we finished our dessert-as-an-appetizer, she said, "You know Mom's on a date tonight, right?"

"What?" I said, almost dropping my glass of milk from the shock. I quickly set it on the counter.

"Yeah," Miranda said. "I heard her talking to Rachel about it last night."

Rachel was Mom's best friend back in Bakersfield.

"Are you sure?" I asked. "Because that doesn't seem like Mom. She's not even officially divorced yet."

Miranda went to the dishwasher and put our dirty glasses inside. "I'm sure. It's a friend of someone at work. They're double-dating. His name is Chris."

The double-dating made me feel a little better. So

maybe it was less like a date and more like hanging out with three friends. Maybe? Hopefully?

Miranda pulled out a saucepan and filled it up with water for the pasta. I went to work frosting the rest of the cupcakes.

"I can't picture either of them with someone else," I told her. "Mom and Dad, I mean. Can you? In my mind, they still go together."

"I know," she said as she turned on the stove burner. "It's just going to take time. But we need to get used to the idea. I mean, she's not going to want to be alone forever."

"But she's not alone," I said. "She has us."

"Juliet, it's not the same."

"What do you mean? Either you're alone or you're not. And she's not." And suddenly, I felt a lot sorrier for Dad.

Miranda tapped me on the shoulder. I turned around and faced her. She looked serious. "Maybe Mom will be happy without a partner. We don't know. But she might also decide she'd be happier with someone. And if she decides that, we need to support her."

"But what if I can't?" I asked. "Like, to me it seems so . . . wrong."

"Actually, it's pretty normal for divorced people to find other people."

I was hardly used to being apart from dad, now I had to start getting used to the idea of them finding other people?

How do you even do that? To me it seemed like taking away a kid's favorite stuffed animal and giving her something like an umbrella in its place. The umbrella might be perfectly nice, but it's still really different. Nothing is going to convince her to be comforted by the umbrella when she misses her stuffed animal.

Miranda grabbed the jar of sauce and twisted the lid. "You want Mom to be happy, right?"

"She has her job, she has us, and she has this cute house at the beach," I pointed out. "That's enough to make her happy."

"She might not think so," Miranda said. "And ultimately, it's up to her, not us."

"I hate the thought of her with someone else," I said. "Maybe it seems normal to you, but not to me." I paused before I mumbled, "The only time I feel normal is when I'm at Emma's house."

"Oh, Pooh," Miranda said. "Makes me sad to hear you say that."

"Like, right now, you know what the Rentons are doing?" I asked. "They're probably sitting down to eat dinner all together. One big, happy family. And here we are, making ourselves dinner because our mom is out on a date with some guy named Chris who could be a big fat jerkface."

Miranda smiled. "I'm sure he's not a jerkface. Mom's friend wouldn't do that to her."

"Whatever," I said as I set the knife down and licked the frosting off my fingers. "It's just not fair."

"Do you want to throw a cupcake at the wall or something?" my sister asked as she put a big handful of noodles into the pan of hot water. "Maybe it'd help you feel better."

"Are you making fun of me?"

She shook her head. "No. Never. Not about something like this. You have every right to feel how you feel."

I thought about throwing a cupcake at the wall, but it didn't seem like that would help much. It might make me feel better for a quick second, but then I'd have to clean up the mess and that was the last thing I wanted to do.

"Do you have any books on your shelf with divorced parents?" I asked.

She replied, "I might. Want me to look when we're done eating?"

"Yes, please."

"You know what, Pooh?" she said.

"What?"

"You're one smart cookie." She smiled. "Or maybe I should say, smart cupcake. And it's going to be okay. You'll see."

Names I don't like

1. *Chris*

That's all I can really think of right now.

Thirty

CRATER LAKE

Last summer, for our family vacation, we drove up to Oregon and went to Crater Lake. That lake is huge. Not only is it the deepest lake in the United States but it's also over five miles across. I'd never seen anything like it. It was big and beautiful and very, very blue. I thought about writing Crayola a letter and telling them they should make a new color blue, model it after the color of the lake, and call it Crater Lake. Brilliant, huh? I mean, in a box of forty-eight, I'd choose Crater Lake over Denim any day. Denim is such a boring color. Denim is everywhere, all the time. But Crater Lake? That's the color you *wish* you had in your life.

Anyway, on the rim of the crater, there's a big brick lodge that has a long porch filled with rocking chairs. After we went on a hike, the four of us sipped cold sodas and rocked while staring out at the gorgeous lake. Maybe that doesn't sound like much fun, doing a whole lot of nothing next to a big body of water, but we all loved it. As we walked back to the car to head to the little country motel we'd be staying at down the road, Mom took my hand in hers, and Miranda's in the other. Without thinking, I reached over and took Dad's hand. We walked like that, our hands swinging and our faces smiling, until we reached the car. Yeah, it sounds like a photo out of *FamilyFun* magazine, something no one in real life would really do, but I swear, we did.

Now, as I lay in bed, waiting for Mom to get home from her double date, I tried to imagine having a perfect day like that with someone other than Dad. And I couldn't do it. To me, it was like trying to imagine a turkey sandwich with cucumber slices instead of pickles.

I thought about getting up and talking to Mom after she got home. I heard her come in, close the front door and lock it, and get a drink of water in the kitchen. But if I'd gotten up, what would I have said? "Hey, Mom, how was your date?" A date I wasn't even supposed to know about, since Miranda only knew because she'd overheard her conversation. Besides, the only answer I would have been happy with was "Horrible. I'm never going on another date as long as I live. You girls are all I need, now and always."

So I stayed in my bed, hoping I'd dream of the perfect afternoon at Crater Lake. (I didn't. I dreamt about climbing a tree and not being able to get down. Basically, the opposite of the perfect afternoon.)

* * *

The next day at school, the hours dragged. All I could think about was whether or not Mr. Dooney would like his surprise. I sat with Emma and her friends again at lunch, but I didn't say much. Being the new kid is not fun. At all. It could have been worse, though. At least I had Emma. When the last bell of the day finally rang, I couldn't get to the front doors fast enough. This time, though, Emma didn't sit with me on the bus. She sat with her friend Shelby, who waved Emma over to her seat as soon as she saw Emma get on. I sunk down in my seat, trying not to sulk. Okay, I was totally sulking. But whatever.

I texted Inca: Hi. I miss you.

She texted back: Miss you, too! Do you like your new school?

My response: It's okay. I might come home this weekend. Maybe we can do something?

She replied with a bunch of emojis of applause. I had forgotten about emojis. I played around and sent her a bunch of random ones: a turtle, a rainbow, a flower, a piece of cake. I imagined her trying to figure out what it all meant, so I decided I better tell her.

Hopefully, I'll see you this weekend and it will be a weekend of happy things.

When we reached our stop, Emma got off first and waited for me.

"Are you ready?" she asked.

"You sure you still want to do this?" I asked.

She scoffed. "What do you mean, do I still want to do

this? Of course! And, hopefully, when it's all over, Mr. Dooney will be a happy man and we'll be the newest members of the Starry Beach Club."

"You didn't tell Shelby about it, did you?" I asked.

She put her backpack on instead of letting it hang from her shoulder. Then she crossed her arms. "Juliet. I would never do that. What's going on? Are you mad that I sat with her? What was I supposed to do? Walk past her and act like I didn't see her frantically waving at me?"

I shook my head. "No. It's fine. I just thought maybe . . . I don't know. Never mind."

She started walking. "If you'd talk to them a little more at lunch, try to get to know them, you'd see they are all super nice."

I laughed. "Talk? How? None of them can stay quiet for more than two seconds."

She stopped and stared at me. "That's mean."

"But it's true."

"No. It's not true. If you'd speak up and say something, they'd listen. I promise. You have to at least try, you know?"

"You don't think I'm trying?"

"Doesn't seem like it to me. Maybe . . . try harder?"

My eyes narrowed and I scowled at her. Had *she* ever been the new kid at school? Had she ever had *anything* bad happen to her, with her wonderful family and her big, beautiful house and her adorable ice cream shop? How could she possibly know what it was like for me? Me and my broken home. My broken heart.

In that moment, it felt like Emma was on one side of Crater Lake and I was on the other. Like she was on the side with the beautiful lodge and I was on the side where there was nothing but wilderness.

"You know," I said, "I think I've decided I'm going to do this Starry Beach Club by myself. You obviously have enough friends. You don't need me or Some Kid. See you later."

I turned around and ran toward my house.

"Juliet!" she called. But I didn't stop. I kept going until I got safely inside. I threw my backpack down, crumpled to the floor, and cried.

Scary things in the wilderness

* *Bears*
* *Wolves*
* *Mountain lions*
* *Big spiders*
* *No food*
* *No bathrooms*

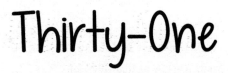

Thirty-One

BIG MISTAKE

I carried the cupcakes in a Rubbermaid container down the boardwalk toward Mr. Dooney's house. My stomach felt like I'd swallowed a bunch of nails. I'd just pushed away the only friend I had in this new town. And I was going to have to try and pull off this tricky wish by myself, without Emma's happy outlook on everything. I tried to imagine her cheering me on.

It's going to be awesome!

He's going to love it!

This is better than melting a wicked witch with a bucket of water!

But it wasn't the same as really having her with me. Especially because whenever I stopped telling myself those things, my brain would just shout really loudly, *This is the dumbest idea ever!*

When I saw Mr. and Mrs. Button standing there,

waiting for me, I felt a little better. At least I had their kind and caring faces to help me get through it.

"Hi," I said when I reached them. "I'm so glad you could come, Mr. Button."

"I figured the fresh air and sunshine would do me good," he said. "And cupcakes will surely help, too."

I felt a tap on my shoulder. "Excuse me?" I turned around. "Are you Juliet?"

An Asian girl stood there with the cutest bob haircut I'd ever seen: thin and wispy with bangs that fell just above her friendly-looking eyes.

"Yeah, I'm Juliet."

"I'm Kari. I'm here to play the piano?"

"Oh, right. Hi! Thank you so much for doing this."

"No problem."

I took a deep breath. "All right. Are we ready?"

"Ready," Mrs. Button said.

There was a white picket fence all the way around the house. I unlatched the gate and led the others up the walkway to the front door. I knocked. When Mr. Dooney came to the door, he said, "Hello, Juliet." He wore khaki pants, a golf shirt, and the same old floppy hat he always had on. He looked past me and said, "Hello, Ray and Flora. So good to see you up and about, Ray."

They both said hello, and then it went quiet. It was my turn to talk, to explain why we were all there. If Emma were with me, she would have said exactly the right thing. But she wasn't there. It was all on me.

I motioned to Kari. "This is Kari and we have a surprise for you."

Mr. Dooney looked confused. "You do?"

I answered. "Yes. We, um, know it's your anniversary today, and since you are probably feeling sad about that, we thought we'd try to cheer you up. Can we come in? And then we'll show you the surprise."

"Certainly," he said, holding the door open for us.

His house smelled good—like gardenias, I thought, as we walked by a big vase of them sitting on a small table in the entryway. To the right was a big, bright room with lots of windows and a black baby grand piano in the center. Kari went over, took a seat on the bench, and took her sheet music out of the folder she'd been carrying. There was also a sofa and a coffee table, so I set the pan of cupcakes on the table and went over to the piano. Mr. and Mrs. Button joined me. Mr. Dooney still stood in the entryway.

"Oh, my," he said, like he knew what was coming. He hesitated a moment and then walked over to stand next to me. Kari looked at me and I gave her a nod. She began to play. Slowly. Carefully. As the four of us stood there, listening to the room fill with sweet, sweet music, it was like time stopped. All that mattered was the lovely song. We stayed as still as statues for the first couple of minutes. It was like we were under a spell. And maybe we were. The spell of "Clair de Lune."

When I finally did move, it was to glance over at Mr. Dooney. I wanted to know if he seemed to be enjoying it. His head was slightly back, his eyes closed, and his lips formed the slightest smile while tears rolled down his cheeks.

Happy and sad, I thought. Just like I'd been so often over the past week. Happy to be at the beach. Happy to have a friend in Emma. But sad to be away from my dad and my friends. I reached over and held Mr. Dooney's hand. It was somehow both rough and soft at the same time. He gave my hand a little squeeze and I kept it there until the song ended. When Kari finished, I gently pulled my hand away so I could clap. We all applauded. Kari stood up, smiled, and gave us a little bow.

I turned to tell Mr. Dooney I really hoped he liked it, but he wasn't next to me anymore. He had snuck out. Disappeared.

"Oh, no," I said softly.

I'd made things worse. He was so upset, he couldn't even stay to talk to us.

"I bet he'll be back," Mrs. Button said. "Let's just give him a minute."

Kari gathered up her sheet music, preparing to leave.

"Thank you," I somehow managed to say. "You're really good. It was beautiful." Only then did I remember the pie Emma had promised her. "I'm sorry, I don't have a pie because Emma's not here. But you can take a couple of cup-cakes if you want."

"Okay, thanks. They look really good."

With cupcakes in hand, she moved toward the door and I knew I needed to be polite and walk her out. I held the door for her as she left and thanked her again. Then I turned and looked at the piano, the cupcakes, and Mr. and Mrs. Button. Suddenly, it all seemed very wrong.

What would I say to Mr. Dooney when he came out, if he even decided to come back out? How could I possibly explain what I was trying to do, when none of it made any sense to me anymore?

There was only one thing I wanted to do right then. And I did it. I opened the door and ran.

Places I'd love to run away to

* *Bakersfield*
* *A castle in Scotland*
* *The Land of Oz*
* *A museum filled with Vincent van Gogh's paintings*
* *Anywhere but here*

Thirty-Two

SCRAMBLED EGGS

I texted Mom and Miranda. I'm going to sit on the beach for a while. Maybe stay and watch the sunset.

Mom asked: Please be safe. What about dinner?

I replied: I'm not hungry. Did you hear from Dad yet? Do I get to go home this weekend?

It took a minute and then she texted: Sorry, honey. He has to work. He feels bad but remember this wasn't a planned visit. He's going to call you in the morning and tell you himself. But since you asked, figured I shouldn't keep it from you.

I stuffed my phone back in my pocket. It seemed like all my parents knew how to do was let me down. No wonder they couldn't even stay married.

I reached down and dug a hole in the sand with my hands as hard and fast as I possibly could. I dug until my arms ached, but it felt good to be doing something besides sitting there feeling bad about everything. Sand covered me and caked my fingernails. But I didn't care. I dug and I dug until I heard from above me, "Digging an anger pit?"

I looked up. It was Emma. I went back to digging and didn't say anything.

She took a seat on the sand next to me. "You probably don't know what that is, so I'll explain. It's a hole where you can put all of your anger. You fill it up, as much anger as you want, and when you're done, you bury it with sand. Instead of being inside of you, the anger is in the ground. And you feel a lot better."

"I've never heard of that," I told her.

"My dad thought of it when the boys were little. Get mad? Feel free to go to the beach and dig a hole for a good, long while. It helps, doesn't it?"

I sat back on my heels, my knees in the sand. My arms felt heavy, like bricks. "Yeah. It does. How come you guys have the best ideas while I have the worst, anyway?"

"You do not have the worst ideas," she said.

"You didn't think we should play the song for Mr. Dooney. But I was sure it would be a good idea. And it wasn't. Not at all."

"Juliet?"

"What?"

"After you left, Mr. Dooney came out to the front room. He said hearing that song on his piano again was one of the happiest moments he's had in a long, long time."

I stared at her. "How do you know? You weren't there."

"I was standing outside. I saw you run off. I wanted to know what happened, so Mr. and Mrs. Button let me in. And Mr. Dooney showed up a minute later. We asked him if he was okay, and he said something like 'I won't lie. It was very bittersweet, because I wish it had been my wife sitting there, playing that lovely song. But mostly, it was one of the happiest moments I've had in a long, long time.'"

"Bittersweet," I repeated.

"Happy and sad," Emma said.

"I love that word," I said. "I think it's a new favorite."

I moved my legs out in front of me and leaned back on my hands. So he hadn't hated it after all. It had probably just made him really emotional and he'd needed a minute to get it together. Like Mrs. Button had said.

"I'm sorry I ran off," I told her. "And I'm sorry for what I said to you earlier. I didn't really mean it. I just—"

"No," she interrupted. "I'm sorry. I shouldn't have said you aren't trying. That wasn't nice. See? Like I told you before, I'm not perfect. Not at all."

"Close," I said.

"You know what happened when I got home from school?" she asked.

"What?"

"My dad yelled at me for leaving the milk on the counter when I left for school. And then Lance yelled at me for going in his room to borrow something without asking him. And then Molly yelled at me because she said I should have

219

bought Kari a nice gift for doing us a favor instead of offering her a pie. She called me an ungrateful brat."

"She did? I think a homemade pie is an awesome gift."

"Right? We still need to bake her one, by the way. Maybe this weekend."

An Irish setter ran up to us, its owner calling out, "Sorry! She's super friendly. Ginger, come here. Come!"

Once Ginger was gone, I crossed my legs and leaned forward. "Since we're sharing family secrets, I guess I can tell you that my mom went on a double date last night. It's so weird."

"Wow. That is weird."

"Yeah. And my dad told my mom I can't come home this weekend because he has to work. It's not fair."

"I'm so sorry, Juliet," Emma said. I could tell from her voice she meant it.

I kept talking. "Maybe your family isn't perfect, but at least you're all together. And at least you have traditions and rules that you know you can always count on."

"You know what you need?" she asked.

"What?"

"A red velvet cupcake. They're so good. We each had one as we listened to Mr. Dooney tell us about his wife. How she made him scrambled eggs for breakfast every morning. How she always thought flies were bees and would run out of the house screaming at the top of her lungs if she saw a fly in the house. How her favorite movie was *The Sound of Music.*"

I felt really sad for Mr. Dooney. "He loved her a lot, didn't he?"

"Yeah. He did. And you know what I think? I think grown-ups need that kind of love. It's different from the kind of love we can give them. I mean, when my mom makes *me* eggs for breakfast, I usually say, 'Can't I have cereal instead?' But my dad? If she makes him breakfast, he's so happy, it's like she's given him a puppy or something."

I laughed. "Eggs and puppies are about as opposite as you can get."

"I know! That's what I mean."

"So, are you saying I should be okay with my mom dating other guys?"

Emma shrugged. "I don't know. I think what I'm saying is everyone deserves the kind of love Mr. Dooney has for his wife. And maybe it just takes some people longer than others to find it. Anyway, can we go and get you a cupcake? Mr. Dooney really wants to thank you."

I sighed. "Okay. But I want to cover this anger pit first. Can you maybe help me?"

"Juliet, do you even have to ask?" She held her hands out wide and sang, *"That's what friends are for."*

Some of my favorite words

* bittersweet—*both pleasant and painful or regretful*
* grateful—*deeply appreciative of kindness or benefits received*
* honest—*good and truthful*
* clair de lune—*French for "light of the moon"*
* puggle—*a cross between a pug and a beagle (and probably the cutest puppy I've ever seen)*

Thirty-Three

JUST DIFFERENT

When we got to Mr. Dooney's house, the Buttons had gone home. But there were two small, wrapped gifts on the porch with tags that said *For Juliet* and *For Emma*. Emma insisted we open them right away. I gasped when I saw the small leather journal, similar to the one Mrs. Button owned. I read the handwritten note.

Juliet,
    Today you and Emma did a kind thing for a dear friend. I thought you each might like to keep your own notebook of beautiful things.
    Love,
    Mrs. Button

"I love it," I told Emma.
"Me, too," she said. "Best gift ever."

And if that wasn't enough, Mr. Dooney told us finding someone to play "Clair de Lune" on the piano was one of the nicest things anyone had ever done for him.

"I was afraid it had made you too sad," I told him.

"Well, I miss her, and with missing comes sadness, yes?" he said. "But the joy I felt was worth the sadness. I love that song, and hearing it again, on our piano that my dear, sweet Patricia loved so much, was a real treat. Truly."

"We're so glad," Emma said. "Is it all right if we have a cupcake, please?"

He laughed. "Help yourself. I certainly can't eat all of those by myself."

Later, on the boardwalk, before we went our separate ways, Emma said, "Make sure you tell Some Kid what Mr. Dooney said about how that was one of the nicest things anyone has ever done for him."

"We did it, didn't we?" I said. "We were clever and creative in coming up with a good idea. Sneaky because he was not expecting that. At all. And diligent. We didn't give up when the first two wishes didn't work out. We kept trying."

Emma put up her hand for a high five. "Yes, we did!"

After I slapped her hand, I asked, "Should I email her tonight?"

"Are you kidding? Yes! And if you hear back, let me know right away, okay?"

"Okay. I guess I'm just nervous. About what happens next."

She laughed. "What happens next is that the mystery is finally solved. It's so exciting!"

We said good-bye and I hurried home. When I walked in the door, Mom shouted from the kitchen, "Oh, good, you're home in time for dinner."

"How'd it go?" Miranda asked me. "Did Mr. Dooney like your surprise?"

"Like what?" Mom asked.

As we ate a dinner of chicken and vegetables with the spicy sauce Laura had given us (it was *really* spicy, but I loved it), I told them all about the afternoon. I showed them the leather notebook Mrs. Button had given me, and told them Mr. Button had even come to hear the song.

Mom sat back in her chair and smiled at me.

"What?" I asked.

"I'm so proud of you, Juliet," she said. "We've only been here a little while and look at the way you've gotten to know people. You're becoming a part of the community, and that is absolutely wonderful. I need to follow your example."

"Maybe if you weren't so busy going on dates," Miranda mumbled.

I was about to take a bite of chicken, but my fork stopped midair. Had my sister just said that? My sister, who'd said I better get used to the idea of Mom dating? Maybe after thinking it over, she realized it wasn't such an easy thing to get used to after all.

"What'd you say?" Mom asked, her smile long gone.

I thought Miranda might say, "Never mind." But she didn't. She repeated what she'd said.

"How do you know I went on a date?" Mom asked.

Miranda wiped her mouth and then set the napkin back in her lap. "I heard you talking to Rachel. I didn't mean to, it's just, these walls are thin. And I heard you say you were going on a double date with someone at work." She motioned at me. "Neither of us can believe you'd do that so soon."

Mom sighed. "Girls, it's really not like it sounds. Yes, I got set up on a date, but I made it very clear that I'm not interested in a relationship right now. The four of us went to dinner, saw a movie, and that was that. I told you I was going out with friends, and that's all it really was."

"Then why'd you call it a date?" I asked.

"I don't know," Mom said, staring at her half-eaten plate of food. "Maybe because I liked the sound of it? For someone like me, who's been married a long time, it's both exciting and terrifying to think about entering the dating world again."

"Do you want to get married again someday?" I asked.

She thought about it for a moment, and then replied, "I think I probably do. But I promise, it's not something I'm going to rush into."

I told them what Emma said, about grown-ups needing the kind of love Mr. Dooney had for his wife. "I guess . . . well, I wish that our love was enough, Mom," I said.

"There are different kinds of love, honey," Mom said.

"That's just the way it is. It's like the love you've easily developed for Emma and her family is different from the love you have for our family. I could be upset about it. Jealous. But I try to tell myself it's different, that's all. Or like your love for art and making lists. You have room in your heart for both, right?"

"Yes," I said. "I do." I realized as she talked that Emma's family was sort of like my lists. Neat. Organized. Fun in an orderly kind of way. My family was like my art. Sometimes light, sometimes dark, sometimes messy, sometimes colorful. Mom was right, they were different. But it didn't make one wrong and one right, or one better than the other.

"Please know this," Mom said. "I love you girls a whole lot. And nothing will ever change that. And I know this is all going to be a big adjustment for a while. But we're going to take it one day at a time, and we'll make it through."

As I sat there looking at my mom and my sister, I didn't feel sad or worried like I had so many times in the past couple of months. I felt . . . calm. Sometimes when I'm painting, early on I'll have moments of panic when I think the piece will never turn out. But I keep going, I keep working on it, and it's almost never as bad as I thought it would be. Sometimes it's even really good. Maybe that's how this whole divorce thing will go, I thought. Maybe having two happy parents who live apart will end up being better than having two unhappy parents who live together.

"Okay, so we don't have to worry about shopping for a wedding gown any time soon?" Miranda teased.

"No," Mom said as she got to her feet. "We're a long way from that, trust me." She turned to go to the kitchen and then stopped. "And, girls, I promise if things appear to be going that way with someone, down the road, like waaaay down the road, you'll be the first people to know. Now, would you mind helping me with these dishes? Then we can have some cupcakes for dessert while we watch a movie together; how's that sound?"

"What movie?" I asked.

"It's Maui time!" Mom said in her best impersonation of The Rock.

It made me laugh. I clapped my hands together. "*Moana!*"

"*Shiny,*" my sister started singing. I joined in. The perfect way to end a sparkly, wish-making kind of day.

Beautiful things #1

* *A song that sounds like wildflowers swaying in the breeze*
* *Cupcakes to say we're thinking of you today*
* *An Irish setter who makes friends wherever she goes*
* *A pit of anger with mysterious powers*
* *Scrambled eggs sprinkled with affection*
* *The word* bittersweet *because so many moments are happy and sad*
* *A friend who is easy to forgive and sweeter than a cupcake*
* *Sparkly, shiny, beautiful love*

Thirty-Four

STILL THINKING

Before I went to bed, I told Mom I needed to do something quickly on the computer. "Okay, but make it fast."

I opened up my email and started typing.

Dear Some Kid,

We did it! We made someone's wish come true. It wasn't obvious, so we had to be clever and creative in coming up with the idea. We had to be sneaky so he'd be surprised. And we had to be diligent because our first wishes didn't work out.

So here's what we did. A really nice old guy lives alone, because his wife passed away. Today would have been their sixtieth wedding anniversary. She used to play her favorite song on their piano, and he hadn't heard it played in his house for five years. So we found someone to play it for him. He said it was very bittersweet, but he loved it. He also said it was one of the nicest things anyone has ever done for him. I'm just glad we could bring him a little joy on what was probably going to be a very long, sad day.

So when can we meet? I'm excited to get the Starry Beach Club going. We'll work together to make more wishes come true, right? I can't wait! I know we haven't met yet, but it already feels like I'm a part of something special. Let's do this, okay? I hope we can meet SOON!

Sincerely yours,

J.J.

Starry Beach Club Member #2?

"Juliet," Mom called. "It's getting late."

"I'm going," I said as I shut the computer down.

After I got into bed, I read until I could hardly keep my eyes open. It was the only way to make myself sleepy, since I was so excited about finally meeting Some Kid.

The next day, Mom and Miranda left the house before I did, as usual. I checked email before school but there was no response. I checked again after school. Still no response.

And that's how it went again the next day, too. I was ready to give up and believe it was some cruel joke when I finally received a response Friday evening.

Hi, J.J.,

Sorry it's taken me so long to write back. I've been trying to figure out the best way for us to meet. Plus, I'm scared. I'm scared that the idea in my head of how this is all going to turn out will be nothing like what happens in real life. What if you guys don't like me? What if you're disappointed in who I am? I keep wondering, who do you want me to be? You've thought about it, I know you have. You asked me to give you a hint, so you're obviously curious.

I know I need to decide. Either we meet or we end it here: A message in a bottle was found, a few emails were exchanged, someone's wish came true, the end.

Still thinking.

Sincerely yours,

Some Kid at the Beach

I couldn't believe it. I typed a response right away.

Dear Some Kid,

You're scared. I get it. It's exactly how I felt before I helped make Mr. Dooney's wish come true. Sometimes it's hard to believe that things will work out for the best. Because sometimes they don't. I know, because my parents split up and some days it seems impossible that things will work out even a tiny bit. But the librarian at my old school told me something we need to remember. He said, "Just like in books, everything usually works out in the end. And if it doesn't, that means you simply haven't reached the end yet."

We already know we have something in common. Vincent! We both love Vincent and his beautiful art. We also know we like the idea of being a part of something special. So let's meet. How about tomorrow (Saturday afternoon) by the bookmobile? Like maybe 1:00? Let's do this! It's going to be fine, you'll see.

Sincerely yours,

J.J.

A couple of minutes later, I had a response.

Okay. See you then.

I texted Emma to let her know. We're meeting Some Kid tomorrow at 1:00 by the bookmobile.

She replied: What if I can't wait that long?

I texted back: You can make me a pie while you're waiting. That will help pass the time!

Beautiful things #2

* *Art, books, and music make the world brighter. They are also the best ingredients for chicken soup for your feelings.*
* *My dad once told me bravery is being scared and doing it anyway.*
* *It's hard being brave, but it usually pays off.*
* *One home here, one home there, two homes are better than none.*
* *Starry night, sunflowers, seascapes—simply stunning.*
* *If I could meet Vincent, the first thing I would say is "Thank you." The second thing I would say is "Maybe sadness doesn't really have to last forever."*

Thirty-Five

TWO WISHES

Emma and I got to the bookmobile early, happy to discover that it was open again. We ran inside to say hello to Mrs. Button. She was at her desk reading a book.

"You're back!" Emma said, practically jumping up and down.

"Hello, girls," she said with a chuckle. "Yes, Mr. Button insisted we not keep people waiting any longer. He's feeling much better and doesn't need me hovering over him every second of the day."

"Such good news," I said.

"Yes," she said, her smile fading. "It is. I just wish . . ."

"What?" Emma asked, when Mrs. Button didn't finish her sentence.

"Well, I suppose the news will get out eventually, so I might as well tell you. We may not be able to keep the bookmobile open much longer."

"Oh, no," Emma said.

"Why not?" I asked.

Mrs. Button got to her feet. "The store changed management and they don't want us here anymore. Not for free, anyway."

"Can you go somewhere else?" I asked.

"You know how it is around here," she said. "Real estate is hard to come by and parking is a nightmare." She paused. "It might be time to pack it in."

I looked over at Emma, and she was shaking her head. "No. You can't. We love this place. I mean, a lot of people love this place. It's small and friendly and easy to get to."

"Isn't there something we can do?" I asked.

Before she could answer, we heard footsteps behind us. We turned to see a girl coming in. She looked familiar.

"Come in, Carmen," Mrs. Button said with a smile. "Don't let us deter you. We were just chatting." She turned to us and said quietly, "We'll have to discuss it another time."

"No problem," Emma said. "Hi, Carmen."

"Hi," she said softly.

Emma motioned me back outside, so I followed. I was still dazed from the news.

"Can you believe it?" Emma asked.

I shook my head. "I know I've only been here a little while, but I love having a place close by to get books. And there's just something about the bookmobile that feels . . ."

What was I trying to say?

"Special?" Emma asked.

"Yes. And maybe Mr. and Mrs. Button make it that way, but whatever it is, I don't want it to close."

"Me either," Emma said as she pulled out her phone. "Five more minutes until one o'clock."

It was gray and cloudy and looked like it might even rain, something I hadn't seen since we'd moved here. I zipped up my hoodie, covering up my sunflower T-shirt. I took in the aroma of fresh-baked bread coming from the nearby store's bakery as I paced, trying not to look like I was searching the street for someone, even though that's exactly what I was doing.

A minute later, Carmen came down the steps of the bookmobile carrying a book. It looked like a picture book, which seemed odd. She was way too old to be reading a picture book.

"Are you guys waiting for something?" Carmen asked.

Emma shrugged. "Just hanging out."

"Oh," Carmen said. "Well, I was wondering . . ." She seemed flustered. I still couldn't figure out why she looked so familiar. Obviously, she went to our school, since Emma knew her. Did I have a class with her? And then, when she shifted the book in her hands and I saw what it was, I remembered. And it all came rushing to me, like a big wave approaching that is obviously going to get you wet.

This was the girl who had been making a sand castle with her brother the day I met Emma. And now, here she was, at the exact moment when we were supposed to meet Some Kid.

I pointed to the book in Carmen's hand, the title, *Camille and the Sunflowers*, now visible. "That looks like a good book."

She turned it around and looked at the cover. "Yes. Someone else has the other Vincent van Gogh book that I wanted to read."

I raised my hand. "Guilty."

Emma moved closer to Carmen, wide-eyed. "It's you? You're Some Kid?"

She nodded and looked at me. "Your bottle washed ashore as soon as you two left. I couldn't help it. I was dying to see what the message said."

I looked at Emma. "How come we didn't think of that?"

"Because we were too busy worrying it might be Henry," she said. "But it's not Henry, it's you!"

Carmen stared at her neon-blue Nikes. "Are you . . . disappointed?"

"Are you kidding?" I asked. "Why would we be disappointed?"

"We're happy it's you!" Emma said, grabbing her hand. "You're nice and normal and—"

"And not Henry," I teased.

Emma laughed. "Yes! I've always wanted to get to know you better."

"Really?" Carmen asked.

"Really!" Emma said. "This is awesome, right, Juliet?"

Carmen gave me a funny look. "Wait. You mean your name isn't J.J.?"

I shook my head. "No. We didn't give our real names. You know, for safety."

"Oh, okay," Carmen said as she nervously twisted a strand of her long, black hair around her finger. "My best friend, she moved away last summer. It's been hard since she left, you know? When I read your letter, it gave me the idea for the club."

"I'm sorry about your friend," I said. "Can I ask you a question?"

"Sure," she replied.

"I'm wondering about Vincent," I said. "What is it that made you like him?"

She smiled. "Ever since we did our own starry night pictures in art lit in fourth grade, I've been obsessed. His art makes me happy. I can't really explain it."

"I get it," I said. "I was just curious."

She continued. "Like I said in my email, at first I thought of the Starry Night Club, but I think we're kinda young for a nightclub."

"I agree," I said, laughing.

"So I kept thinking," Carmen said, "and came up with the Starry Beach Club. But if you guys have another idea . . ."

"No," Emma said. "We love it." She looked at me. "Right?"

"Right," I said. "It's perfect."

"I think we should celebrate," Emma said. "And then we need to figure out what we do next. Wish-wise, I mean."

"You know, I have an idea," I said.

Emma pointed to the bookmobile while she stuck out her bottom lip. Pouty face. "I bet it's the same idea I have."

Carmen looked from Emma to me. "What is it?"

"Don't worry," I said. "We'll tell you all about it. It's going to take a lot of cleverness and creativity, that's for sure."

"Ice cream might help," Emma suggested. "What do you say?"

"Sweet!" I said.

"And then maybe we can all go to my house and make a pie?" Emma said. She turned to Carmen. "Someone did us a favor in making Mr. Dooney's wish come true. I promised her a pie."

"All right," Carmen said. "I'll just have to borrow a phone and tell my mother that I'll be gone all afternoon."

We started walking back toward the Frozen Spoon. "Do you live around here?" Emma asked.

"No," Carmen replied. "We live in an apartment over by the middle school. But I walk here all the time. It's only a couple of miles."

The way she said it, I realized how lucky I was to live so close to the beach. Grandma and Grandpa had owned the little red house for a really long time. They probably weren't charging us much rent to live there, either.

As we walked, the gray clouds parted and the sun came out. No rain after all. Maybe this place wasn't Bakersfield, but it was all right, and I realized I'd grown to like it. Maybe even love it a little bit. I fished the Tic Tacs out of my pocket, took one, and passed them to Emma. She took one and passed them to Carmen.

"Maybe we don't have a secret handshake, but we have mints and fresh breath," Emma said.

"My kind of club," Carmen said as she passed the mints back to me.

I smiled. "Same."

I bet most people have more than one wish they keep tucked away in their hearts like I do. Some come true and some don't. That's just the way it works. When things don't go the way you want, you keep wishing. And maybe one day, out of the blue, one magically comes true.

I thought of the list I'd made before we moved here. A list of all the things I wanted to do at the beach, to try and make myself more excited about my new home.

"Do you think someday we could fly kites on the beach?" I asked. "And maybe roast marshmallows over a bonfire? When we're not busy helping make wishes come true, I mean."

"Sounds good to me," Carmen said. "I've never eaten a roasted marshmallow before."

"No way," Emma said. "We have to fix that."

When we arrived at the shop a couple of minutes later, I said, "Before we go inside, can I take our picture?"

"Ooh, good idea," Emma said as she leaned up against the doorjamb. "We need to remember this day—the first day of the Starry Beach Club. Are you going to frame it and put it next to your bed?"

I got my phone out and held it out in front of us as we squished our heads together. "No. I think I'll tape it inside my notebook of beautiful things."

We put on our wonderful selfie smiles and I took the photo. Then Emma started singing, *"You've got a friend in me."*

"I love that movie!" Carmen said. "Woody and Buzz are so funny."

Emma sang it again and we joined in. Then we laughed.

Want to know one thing that's even better than birds with joy sprinkled on their wings? Friends who are brilliant and bursting with life and make you feel like you're a part of something special. I didn't have to live in a painting. All I had to do was find people who made me feel like I did. And lucky for me, I had.

"You know what?" I said before Emma opened the door. "I think we actually made *two* people's wishes come true this week."

"We did?" Emma asked. "Whose?"

I smiled like she'd just handed me a painting by Vincent. "Mine."

"Um, make that three wishes," Carmen said, her brown eyes practically sparkling.

"We better not stop now," Emma said. "We're on a roll!"

Acknowledgments

This story was partly inspired by events in my own life. So first and foremost, I want to say thank you to the Runyon family for "adopting" me as a fifth child for a while in elementary school. And thanks to the Vorderstrasse family for allowing me to be a part of your family for a time in high school. Words can't really express how much I appreciate your kindness, generosity, and most of all, your love. Please know I cherish the memories I have with all of you and that you will always hold a special place in my heart.

Thanks, as always, to Amanda Maciel and Abby McAden for all of their work on my behalf. Thanks as well to Scholastic Clubs and Scholastic Fairs—seeing my books in your beautiful flyers and in schools across the country is such an honor. I want to specifically thank Ann Marie Wong and Jana Haussmann for your incredible support. I really appreciate you! Yaffa Jaskoll, your cover and page designs rock and I'm so grateful for your work. And a huge thank you to my fabulous agent, Sara Crowe. You really get my work and I feel so blessed to have traveled this path with you the past ten years.

A shout-out to librarians and teachers who work tirelessly to get the right books into the right hands. Your work matters—it matters so much.

And finally, thank you to every person who has bought my books, shared my books, talked about my books, and/or read my books. I couldn't do this without you. So thank you, dear reader. A million times, thank you!

The trip of a lifetime . . .

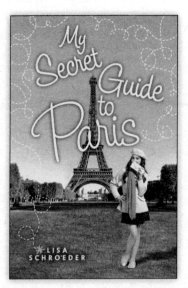

Nora loves everything about Paris, from the Eiffel Tower to *chocolat chaud*. Of course, she's never actually been there—she's only visited through her grandma Sylvia's stories. And just when they've finally planned a trip together, Grandma Sylvia is suddenly gone, taking Nora's dreams with her.

Nora is crushed. She misses her grandmother terribly, but she still wants to see the city they both loved. So when Nora finds letters and a Paris treasure map among her grandma Sylvia's things, she dares to dream again . . .

She's not sure what her grandma wants her to find, but Nora knows there are wonderful surprises waiting for her in Paris. And maybe, amongst the croissants and *macarons*, she'll even find a way to heal her broken heart.

A little piece of magic . . .

When Phoebe finds a beautiful antique at a flea market, she's not sure if it's as valuable as it looks. But inside she discovers something truly amazing—a letter, written during World War II, from a young girl to her sister who's been evacuated from London. The letter includes a "spell" for bringing people closer together: a list of clues leading all through the city. Each stop along the way adds up to magic.

Phoebe is stunned. Not only has she found a priceless piece of history, but the letter is exactly what she needs—she's also separated from her sister, though not by distance. Alice leaves for university soon, but in the meantime, she wants nothing to do with Phoebe. They used to be so close. Now that Phoebe has this magical list, maybe she can fix everything! That is, unless she accidentally makes everything worse instead . . .

Follow your heart . . .

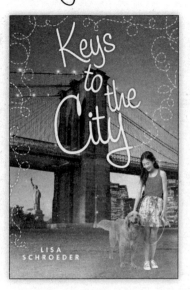

$\mathcal{L}$indy can't wait for summer. Her family has moved to a beautiful old brownstone in New York City, where her parents are opening a bed-and-breakfast. She'll meet new people, visit her friends in Brooklyn, and spend lots of time curled up with a good book.

Or so she thought. Right before school ends, Lindy's class gets a summer assignment: to find their "true passion." Something they love *and* that they're good at. Something special. Their *thing*.

So much for a relaxing summer.

Then some new friends offer to help Lindy explore the city and go on adventures to find her passion. Lindy isn't sure it'll work, but New York is a big place. If the city can help Lindy unlock her potential, maybe the key to the perfect summer will be hers after all . . .

Lisa Schroeder is the author of several books for young readers, including *Keys to the City*, *Sealed with a Secret*, *My Secret Guide to Paris*, the Charmed Life series, the It's Raining Cupcakes trilogy, and *The Girl in the Tower*. Lisa is a native Oregonian and lives in Beaverton with her husband and two sons. When she's not writing, you will probably find her reading, walking the dog, or baking yummy treats—and online at lisaschroederbooks.com.